DEA

Only halfway through ~~~~~~~~~~~~~~
elbows and knees bled p~~~~~~~~. But so far there was no
sign of Sis-ki-dee. Yet where else could the renegade be?
He wasn't in either of the cars Touch the Sky had checked,
nor was he on the train. That left only the bottom. But with
Sis-ki-dee, normal logic didn't apply.

Touch the Sky continued his grim journey, frustrated
because he felt he was wasting his time, yet knowing it had
to be done. Then, above the singing came new sounds: a
boy's piercing scream of abject fear, fast footsteps pounding
through the coach above him, and the sudden explosion of
a gun! Sis-ki-dee had struck!

Touch the Sky's heart crawled into his throat. Flinging
all caution to the wind, the warrior rolled out from under
the coach, leapt to his feet, and sprinted toward the occupied
car. Immediately the renegades opened fire on him.
Crouching to minimize the target, Touch the Sky sang his
death song even as he hurtled toward the coach.

The *Cheyenne* Series:
- # 1: ARROW KEEPER
- # 2: DEATH CHANT
- # 3: RENEGADE JUSTICE
- # 4: VISION QUEST
- # 5: BLOOD ON THE PLAINS
- # 6: COMANCHE RAID
- # 7: COMANCHEROS
- # 8: WAR PARTY
- # 9: PATHFINDER
- #10: BUFFALO HIDERS
- #11: SPIRIT PATH
- #12: MANKILLER
- #13: WENDIGO MOUNTAIN
- #14: DEATH CAMP
- #15: RENEGADE NATION

16
CHEYENNE

ORPHAN TRAIN
JUDD COLE

LEISURE BOOKS **NEW YORK CITY**

A LEISURE BOOK®

February 1996

Published by

Dorchester Publishing Co., Inc.
276 Fifth Avenue
New York, NY 10001

If you purchased this book without a cover you should be aware that this book is stolen property. It was reported as "unsold and destroyed" to the publisher and neither the author nor the publisher has received any payment for this "stripped book."

Copyright © 1996 by Dorchester Publishing Co., Inc.

All rights reserved. No part of this book may be reproduced or transmitted in any form or by any electronic or mechanical means, including photocopying, recording or by any information storage and retrieval system, without the written permission of the Publisher, except where permitted by law.

The name "Leisure Books" and the stylized "L" with design are trademarks of Dorchester Publishing Co., Inc.

Printed in the United States of America.

Prologue

In the year the white man's winter count called 1840, a Northern Cheyenne warrior was born to face a great but bloody destiny.

His original Cheyenne name was lost forever after a bluecoat ambush near the North Platte killed his father and mother and 30 other Cheyennes riding under a truce flag. The squalling infant was left the lone survivor after his life was spared by the lieutenant in charge. He was taken back to the Wyoming river-bend settlement of Bighorn Falls near Fort Bates. There, he was adopted by John Hanchon and Hanchon's barren young wife, Sarah.

Owners of the town's thriving mercantile store, the Hanchons named the child Matthew and loved him as their own son in spite of occasional hostile looks and remarks from other settlers. But their affection couldn't save Matthew when he turned 16 and made the mistake of falling in love with Kristen, daughter of the wealthy and hidebound rancher Hiram Steele.

Steele had Matthew severely beaten when he caught the Cheyenne youth and Kristen in their secret meeting place. The rancher also warned Matthew that the next time he caught him with his daughter, the youth would be killed. Frightened for Matthew's safety, Kristen lied and told her father that she never wanted to see Matthew again. Still, Matthew's love for his parents and Kristen kept him in Bighorn Falls.

But Seth Carlson, an arrogant young lieutenant from Fort Bates, was also in love with Kristen. He altered Matthew's life forever when he issued an ultimatum: Either Matthew left Bighorn Falls for good or his parents would lose their lucrative contract with Fort Bates—the backbone of their business.

Thus began the odyssey of the brave but lonely Cheyenne youth trapped between two worlds and welcome in neither. His heart sad but determined, Matthew set out for the up-country of the Powder River, Cheyenne territory.

Matthew was immediately captured by braves from Chief Yellow Bear's Northern Cheyenne camp. His clothing, manners, and speech marked him as an enemy. Declared a spy for the blue-bloused soldiers, the youth was tortured

Orphan Train

and sentenced to die. But just as a young brave named Wolf Who Hunts Smiling was about to gut him, old Arrow Keeper intervened.

The tribe shaman and protector of the sacred Medicine Arrows, Arrow Keeper had recently experienced an epic vision. His vision foretold that the long-lost son of a great Cheyenne chief would return to his people—and that the youth would lead his people in one last, great victory against their enemies. That youth would be known by the distinctive mark of the warrior, the same birthmark Arrow Keeper spotted buried past the youth's hairline: a mulberry-colored arrowhead.

Keeping all that information to himself to protect the youth from jealous tribal enemies, Arrow Keeper used his influence to spare the prisoner's life. Arrow Keeper's actions infuriated the cunning Wolf Who Hunts Smiling and his fierce older cousin, Black Elk.

Black Elk, the tribe's war leader, was jealous of the glances cast at the tall young stranger by Honey Eater, daughter of Chief Yellow Bear. And Wolf Who Hunts Smiling had turned his heart to stone against all whites without exception. To him, Matthew was only a make-believe Cheyenne who wore white man's shoes, spoke the paleface tongue, and showed his emotions like the woman-hearted whites.

Arrow Keeper buried Matthew's white name forever, calling him Touch the Sky. But acceptance did not come as easily as the youth's new name. At first, as Touch the Sky trained to be a warrior, he was humiliated at every turn. Nor did his enemies within the tribe cease their relentless campaign to prove Touch the Sky was a spy for the whites.

By dint of sheer determination, guts, and the cunning he learned from whites, Touch the Sky not only became the greatest warrior of the Shaiyena nation, but also made progress in the shamanic arts, thanks to Arrow Keeper's training. His fighting skill and courage won him more and more followers, including the ever loyal brave Little Horse.

But with each victory, Touch the Sky's enemies managed to turn appearances against him, to suggest that he still carried the white man's stink, which brought the tribe bad luck and scared off the buffalo. And although the entire tribe knew that Touch the Sky and Honey Eater were desperately in love, Honey Eater was forced into a loveless marriage with Black Elk, who had since chafed in jealous wrath, plotting revenge against Touch the Sky and Honey Eater.

Then, after the mysterious disappearance of Arrow Keeper, Wolf Who Hunts Smiling killed Black Elk and accused Touch the Sky of the murder. Having formed secret alliances with Comanche and Blackfoot renegades, Wolf Who Hunts Smiling established his terrifying Renegade Nation atop Wendigo Mountain. He planned to raise the lance of leadership over the entire Cheyenne nation and lead a war of extermination against the whiteskin settlers.

Only one obstacle prevented his final bid for absolute power: the tall brave named Touch the Sky.

Chapter One

"Brother," Little Horse said, nodding toward the peaks of the distant Sans Arcs Mountains, "the worst trouble in the world lives there."

Touch the Sky followed his friend's gaze. The two Cheyenne braves sat their ponies on the spine of a long ridge not far beyond the point the whites called the hundredth meridian, where the rainfall began to slacken and tall grass gave way to the short-grass prairie.

To the north, the Sans Arcs thrust their snow-capped spires into the soft blue belly of the sky. Behind them to the east, Touch the Sky could make out the confluence of the Powder and Little Powder Rivers, where Chief Gray Thunder's Cheyenne people made their summer camp each year after the spring melt. To the west and south,

Orphan Train

the Cheyenne and Sioux hunting grounds stretched in an unbroken, rolling expanse.

But Touch the Sky kept his eyes trained toward the San Arcs range, especially the tallest peak of all, which was slightly isolated from the others: Wendigo Mountain.

"You speak straight arrow, brother," Touch the Sky finally said. "The worst trouble in the world lives there indeed. And all the signs tell me that same trouble will soon once again make our world a hurting place."

Touch the Sky was lean, straight, and tall, with a strong, hawk nose and keen black eyes. His hair hung in loose black locks except where it was cut off close above the brows to keep his vision clear. It was the Moon When the Geese Fly South, the beginning of the cold moons, and both braves had abandoned their light breechclouts for buckskin shirts and leggings. Both braves also wore leather bands around their left wrists for protection from the slap of their bowstrings.

Little Horse watched his friend carefully, saying nothing. When Touch the Sky spoke of signs, Little Horse knew he was not speaking figuratively. After all, was it not that tall brave whom old Arrow Keeper had marked out to replace him as the tribe's shaman and keeper of the sacred medicine arrows? Those four stone-tipped arrows symbolized the fate of the tribe. Old Arrow Keeper had mysteriously disappeared, and it was up to Touch the Sky to protect those arrows with his life, to keep them forever sweet and clean.

"What have you seen, brother?" Little Horse asked softly.

Touch the Sky finally broke his long gaze toward Wendigo Mountain, meeting his loyal friend's eyes squarely. "What have I seen, buck? You mean, what manner of vision was placed over my eyes?"

Little Horse nodded. Built small but solid, the warrior rode a tough little piebald. Touch the Sky sat a medicine-hat mustang—a light-colored pony covered with black speckles. Those ponies were considered good luck by Indians.

"Never mind medicine visions," Touch the Sky said. "It needs not the shaman eye to see certain things. We have seen Big Tree, the best pony warrior among the Comanche Nation, lead his braves to that mountain. We have seen Sis-ki-dee, the crazy-by-thunder Blackfoot marauder, lead his murdering Contrary Warriors to that mountain. And do you need the High Holy Ones to tell you that the worst traitor in our camp, Wolf Who Hunts Smiling, has crossed his lance with those of Big Tree and Sis-ki-dee?"

Little Horse nodded. "As you say, all this is true enough. But, brother, I know you. You would not have ridden out on this scouting mission for all those familiar reasons. What new sign has been revealed?"

Touch the Sky's lips formed a grim, determined slit as he again stared toward the mist-shrouded slopes of Wendigo Mountain. Little Horse was right, although their scouting mission had failed to reveal any useful information.

"Straight words, Cheyenne. I have indeed had a vision. In that vision, the sacred arrows lay on a stump. To the left of the stump was assembled our entire tribe—only Gray Thunder was absent and Wolf Who Hunts Smiling held the common pipe."

At those words, a bit of color drained from Little Horse's face because only the tribe's chief could hold the common pipe.

"To the right of the stump," Touch the Sky said, "stood our little band: you, Tangle Hair, Two Twists, and myself. And, buck, there was blood on the arrows."

Cold blood surged into Little Horse's face, and he lost the rest of his color. There was no symbolism more potent to a Cheyenne than the image of bloody medicine arrows. The twin-horned nature of the vision was perfectly clear to Little Horse. Not only was Gray Thunder's tribe in grave danger, but Touch the Sky and his most loyal followers faced the worst fate known to an Indian: permanent banishment from the Cheyenne tribe.

"Arrow Keeper once told me," Touch the Sky said, "that a Cheyenne without a tribe is a dead Cheyenne. This scouting mission revealed nothing, and we must return to camp before our enemies stir up new treachery in our absence. But

I trust the dream signs. Whatever new scheme Wolf Who Hunts Smiling and his murdering allies have in store, it is meant to either kill us or have us banished forever."

Their sister the sun had just gone to her resting place when the two braves returned to their camp at the fork where the Little Powder joined the Powder.

From a distant rise, the camp was a welcome sight. The tipis, erected in circles by clans, were covered with tanned buffalo hides. Many had worn so thin they were bright from the light of the fire pits within. Dark plumes curled out the smoke holes.

Indian camps remained lively far into the night. A group of adolescent boys played a hoop-and-pole game by the light of a huge fire; groups of braves stood before their clan or soldier society lodges, smoking and reciting past coups; squaws huddled over their cooking tripods, preparing the evening meal. The Cheyenne, more than any other tribe, relied on dogs for camp security, and those animals set up a friendly racket as the two friends rode closer.

Touch the Sky paid scant attention to all the familiar sights, sounds, and smells. Instead, his worried eyes automatically cut to a lone tipi built on a ridge between the clan circles and the river.

A smile touched his lips when he saw an elongated shadow reflected from within. But that smile faded as he glanced around the rest of the camp.

"Brother," he said thoughtfully to Little Horse as they quartered around toward the huge common corral, "a thing troubles me. Where are Wolf Who Hunts Smiling and Medicine Flute? They rode out two sleeps ago, and still they are gone. I hoped our scouting mission would tell us something. I would rather have a rattlesnake in my sleeping robe than know those two are up to secret treachery."

They turned their ponies loose in the rope corral and pulled their buffalo-hair hackamores. As they returned to the central camp clearing, Touch the Sky again felt a deadly tension dividing his camp. It was reflected in the reactions of those braves who noticed them. Those who belonged to the Cheyenne soldier society known as the Bow Strings, led by Spotted Tail, greeted both youths warmly, as did many of the camp elders.

But the braves who followed Lone Bear, leader of the Bull Whip soldier society, avoided eye contact with Touch the Sky and Little Horse or threw sly, slanted glances at them, muttering insults. But not one was foolish enough to speak too loudly since those two warriors fought like 20 men.

"Why does Lone Bear go on pretending to be a troop leader?" Little Horse said. "It is common knowledge that he plays the fawning dog for

Wolf Who Hunts Smiling and this pretend shaman, Medicine Flute."

Touch the Sky nodded, his attention again focused on that lone tipi between the clan circles and the river. Little Horse noticed, and a fond smile touched his lips briefly.

Touch the Sky said, "Wolf Who Hunts Smiling has made it the goal of his life to convince the rest that I murdered his cousin so that I could marry Honey Eater. He would turn their hearts to stone against me."

"Straight words, buck. Yet it was he who killed the one who may not be mentioned. Just as it is he who conspires with our enemies on Wendigo Mountain, all the time preaching to the people about loyalty to the Red Nation."

Neither brave had pronounced the dead Black Elk's name since Indians believed the dead would answer upon hearing their names spoken. Little Horse went off to find their companions Tangle Hair and Two Twists while Touch the Sky angled toward that lone, orange-glowing tipi.

Despite the silence of the brave's elkskin moccasins in the deep grass, Honey Eater stepped outside the entrance flap even before he lifted it.

Seeing her softly backlit by the fire blazing within made Touch the Sky pause on the edge of a breath and go completely still at such beauty. The fairest flower in all the meadows, Arrow Keeper had once called the willow-slender maiden. While most of the young women in the tribe wore glittery beads, buttons, or shells in their hair, her long black hair was braided only with petals of fresh white columbine. Her skin was the color of her favorite food, wild honey.

"Maiyun has given you to me for another night," she said, greeting him, and those two lovers both felt her words deeply.

Against all odds, and in the face of deadly opposition, they had finally exchanged vows during the squaw-taking ceremony. Death stalked Touch the Sky like a vindictive bear every day. Honey Eater did indeed attribute his safe return to God's will—and her warrior's skill and bravery since his coup feathers trailed the ground and he sat behind no man in council.

Long habit made him pull her away from the light and into the cool darkness away from the tipi. "It has come to this. I fear murder attempts in our very camp! As Wolf Who Hunts Smiling has already proven, murderers sometimes miss and kill the wrong person. When we go inside, the fire must be put out immediately. No shadows for them to aim at."

"If they kill you," Honey Eater said, laying one cheek against his scarred chest and feeling the hard muscles, "I hope I die with you."

"Enough peyote talk, little one. You sound like a boasting warrior. Better to talk of living with me. That is what I mean for us to do. I understand your fear, and I share it. But fear is only a mean pony, and even mean ponies can be gentled. I know the strength in you, just as I knew your father, the greatest peace chief of all Northern Cheyennes.

"We will live, Honey Eater! We have turned our hearts to stone toward the murdering, lying traitors who follow Wolf Who Hunts Smiling and the Bull Whips. The fight is coming, and it will be hard. But we were marked out by the High Holy Ones to fight this battle. Maiyun, the Good Supernatural, has His own battle plan. Now give over with this pensive, fearful manner. When all the stones melt so too will my love for you. Let them kill us. We will have this night among others and that is reason enough for me to fight."

Honey Eater felt hot tears spring to her eyes. For a long moment they held each other close and tight, sharing their determination and their need. Since he had taught her to like the white man's custom of kissing, Honey Eater brought velvet-soft lips to his hungry mouth.

"Let us go put out one fire," she whispered, "and start another—the three of us."

Despite the physical weariness weighing down his muscles, Touch the Sky immediately noticed Honey Eater's last four words. He drew back and held her out at arm's length, studying her pretty, high-boned face in the moonlight. Modestly, her eyes ran from his, but a proud smile divided her face. Touch the Sky could say nothing since a welling of deep emotion suddenly pinched shut his throat.

Orphan Train

"I am giving you a child," she whispered. "I know you thought I never would, and I believed this, too. When I did not give he who is gone the son he so desperately wanted, the women of his Panther Clan said that I am not a woman, but a witch. Everyone knows that witches have no wombs. Now I understand. Because I did not love him, Maiyun spared me the horror of bearing his child."

Though she had not named Black Elk, Honey Eater made the cutoff sign for speaking of the dead. She would not risk a curse on her unborn child in that vulnerable moment.

"I need no child to love you," he said quietly, finally trusting his voice. "Nor do I care if our babe is buck or doe. The Day Maker has put this spark of life in you, and we will nurse it to being as carefully as Sister Bear watches her cubs. But, little Honey Eater, do you understand the importance of keeping this thing quiet for as long as possible?"

Honey Eater did not need the urgent tone in his voice to apprise her of the danger. "Husband, have I not seen how you surround our sleeping robes with dried pods and sticks at night? Do you believe that I am blind, that I do not know that you have several braves you trust watching me closely when you leave camp?

"Of course my pregnancy must be kept a secret, tall warrior. I have given it much thought. You must of course tell Little Horse, Tangle Hair, and Two Twists. Those three would face the Wendigo with empty bows if you told them they must. Our secret is safe with them. And I must tell my Aunt Sharp Nosed Woman since no woman can face this important thing alone. I do not fear for myself, but for our child. Sharp Nosed Woman loves me true. She will keep our secret close to her heart."

Touch the Sky approved her decision with a nod. Again Honey Eater demonstrated the great wisdom that matched her great beauty. Touch the Sky held her close for a long moment, then slowly led her through the darkness back toward their lodge.

But the good news carried with it the potential for great tragedy. It reminded Touch the Sky of a hard lesson of his life: The more things a man loved, the more places his enemies could hurt him. Nor could he forget the ominous medicine dream he had described to Little Horse.

So two questions gnawed at him, making his nape tingle as his shaman sense warned him: Where was Wolf Who Hunts Smiling? And what was he up to?

Chapter Two

"This is the spot where we will send the iron horse to its destruction," Wolf Who Hunts Smiling said.

The Cheyenne brave had halted his two companions in the low country just north of the place where the Platte River joined the Laramie River. The paleface town called Register Cliffs lay just out of sight behind a wooded bluff.

The three Indians swung down from their mounts and tethered them in the lush bunchgrass with long strips of rawhide. Wolf Who Hunts Smiling led the other two closer to the tracks of the Kansas-Pacific Railroad.

"See there," Wolf Who Hunts Smiling said, "how the rails curve coming out of this long defile? The walls of the defile are sloped. We place the thunder pack on the rails just as the curve begins. That way, the iron horse will be blown from the tracks. But the lodges on wheels, in which the children will be riding, will only be blown off the tracks and come to rest against the walls of the defile. The children will not be hurt."

Wolf Who Hunts Smiling was small, but sinew tough, with a wily face and swift, furtive eyes that watched every movement around him. Like Roman Nose of the Southern Cheyenne Dog Soldiers, he preached contempt for the hoary-headed elders who advised cooperation with white men. And because treachery was his favorite weapon, he had learned to watch for the ever expected attack.

"It will be a simple matter," he said, "to bring all your men down from Wendigo Mountain with their horses. Each man takes a child and rides back to camp with it. If there are extra children, we can simply let the hair faces rescue them. Indeed, we will have plenty for a generous ransom. The palefaces will pay much for the return of their children."

The brave's two companions had remained silent for some time, letting their Cheyenne ally explain his new plan to get paleface money for weapons and powder and ball, for good tobacco and coffee and sugar. These three fearsome renegades had brought a new terror to the buffalo country. Wendigo Mountain had become home to Wolf Who Hunts Smiling's Renegade Nation.

Orphan Train

The huge Comanche named Big Tree spoke up. He wore his hair parted in the middle and just long enough to brush behind his ears. He was still a young man, but the sere sun of his Southwest homeland had lined his face like the clay bed of a dried-up river.

"Buck, we have only two thunder packs left. I am loath to waste one on this scheme. What if there are no children on the train?"

Big Tree spoke in the curious mix of Cheyenne and Sioux that was common on the Great Plains. His words were approved by the third brave, a Blackfoot named Sis-ki-dee, who nodded his support.

"The children will be aboard," Wolf Who Hunts Smiling said. "News has come by way of Moccasin Telegraph from the Lakota reservation at Roaring Horse Creek to the east: one entire wheeled lodge full of children."

Sis-ki-dee threw back his head and roared with laughter. Big brass rings dangled from slits in his ears; heavy copper brassards protected his upper arms from enemy lances and axes. His face, once ruggedly handsome, was badly marred by smallpox scars. In defiance of the long-haired tribe that had expelled him, he and all of his contrary warriors wore their hair cropped ragged and short. Even with no danger in sight, he carried his .44-caliber North and Savage rifle in a buckskin sheath.

"This is peyote talk!" he said scornfully. "Of

course I would support this plan if indeed paleface children were for the taking. But, bucks, no tribe, red or white, values anything more than its children.

"Look at Big Tree here. No tribe on the Plains is considered more coldhearted than the Red Raiders of the Comanche Nation. Yet I have seen Big Tree's face soften like a woman's at sight of a child."

"Do you call me a woman?" Big Tree said with menacing quiet.

Again Sis-ki-dee roared with mirth. "No need to rise on your hind legs and make the he-bear roar, buck! I do not question your manhood, nor would I eagerly cross my lance with yours. I only mean to make a point: If even a man as hard as you gentles around children, how must the weak palefaces feel? They would not abandon their children to travel beyond the Great Waters like this, alone and unprotected. If children are on that iron horse, there will be soldiers, too."

Big Tree and Wolf Who Hunts Smiling exchanged secret glances when Sis-ki-dee spoke of valuing children. They had both heard the story about Sis-ki-dee grabbing a paleface infant around both ankles and slamming it to death against a tree right in front of the horrified mother.

"No blue blouses," Wolf Who Hunts Smiling said. "I have sent a courier to check with Seth Carlson at the soldiertown called Fort Bates. He is not our ally, but you know how deep his hatred for Woman Face is. He encourages my plan so long as we can heap the blame on Woman Face. He swears there are no soldiers on the wheeled lodge, just one unarmed civilian serving as an escort."

Sis-ki-dee and Big Tree instantly recognized the name Woman Face as a reference to the tall Cheyenne shaman known as Touch the Sky. Wolf Who Hunts Smiling had dubbed his enemy Woman Face soon after the brave raised by white men was captured by the Powder River tribe. Touch the Sky's habit of showing his feelings in his face had earned the scorn of the Cheyenne warriors.

"If the little eagle chief named Carlson has verified this thing," Big Tree said thoughtfully, "then perhaps it is true. Surely, if any hair face hates the tall one, it is Carlson."

"I have ears for this," Wolf Who Hunts Smiling said, flashing the furtive smile that earned him his name. "As for me, I have raised my battle-ax against Woman Face until death! In front of my tribe's best warriors, I walked between him and the fire. Now I must make good on my promise and kill him."

"Familiar words," Sis-ki-dee said scornfully. "Big Tree here shot a long arrow through Woman Face, skewering him, pinning him to the ground. You, wily wolf, set loose a grizzly bear on him, had him bullwhipped, and hung from a pole by hooks through his chest. And I have failed to send him under with bullets, boulders, and even a mountain lion."

"Spoken straight," Wolf Who Hunts Smiling said, raising high the green canvas pack with its lethal charge of nitroglycerin.

Several moons earlier, they had stolen several more like it from a blue-blouse supply train. With those formidable munitions, they had nearly succeeded in seizing the mining camp of Touch the Sky's white friend, Caleb Riley. But they were stymied yet again by the Cheyenne who had arrived among his people wearing shoes and mounting his horse from the left side, the white man's side.

"We have all of us failed to kill him," Wolf Who Hunts Smiling said. "Yet die he must! I hate Woman Face more than I hate the Pawnees and Crows and turncoat Utes! May he die hard of the yellow vomit!

"But we must have done with this he-bear talk. Talk will not kill him. There is only one way left, and the blue blouse called Seth Carlson has struck upon it. We must paint Touch the Sky so black, in legend and rumor, that the Red Nation will expel him. Once we have destroyed the iron horse and seized the paleface children, the clever Medicine Flute waits back at camp to help me plant the story of Touch the Sky's guilt for this heinous crime. We will not only supply our new camp from this mission, but destroy our worst enemy in the eyes of my people. When I am ready to seize control of my tribe and join you on Wendigo Mountain, he will be smoke behind us."

Big Tree and Sis-ki-dee both nodded. When the Cheyenne thrust out his red-streamered lance, they each laid one hand on it.

"I swear this thing," Wolf Who Hunts Smiling said solemnly, "and this place hears me. From where we stand now to the place where the sun goes down, Woman Face has no place to hide!"

Even as he finished speaking, a steam whistle blasted in the distance, approaching from the east. The nitro packs were percussion detonated, and the sudden weight of locomotive wheels would unleash the force of the Wendigo. Wolf Who Hunts Smiling hurried toward the tracks and knelt to place the thunder pack.

"Back in the land of steady habits, we ain't worth a plugged peso to nobody," Hush Cochran said. "That's how's come they're sending us to all these one-horse towns out west. Hell, we're just orphans. Them farmers'll work us like mules."

Esther Buchanan looked shocked and promptly turned around in her seat to grab the 13 year old's arm. She had been employed by the Children's Aid Society of New York City because she had a no-nonsense manner and the grip of an eagle.

"Hush Cochran, you shut your mouth! This is the last time I'm warning you. If you keep talking like that to the younger children, I'll make you ride all the way to the end of the line. Then you can fend for yourself in wild Indian country."

"Huh," the lad muttered in a surly tone, pushing his battered bowler hat back even farther on his head. An unruly shock of wheat-colored hair covered most of his forehead. Behind him, the passenger car was filled with more children, ranging from five year olds up to nearly Hush's age.

"I ain't scared a no damn Injuns," Hush said boldly.

"Aw, bunk. You ain't never seen no Injuns," 11 year old Tommy Truesdale said from across the aisle.

When Tommy was still an infant, his 16-year-old mother had been found frozen to death in a Boston doorway. She had removed most of her clothing to protect Tommy. After running away from an orphanage at age ten, he had become a shoe-shine boy until he was recruited by a thief to be a moll buzzer—a pickpocket who specialized in stealing from women. Like many of the older children on board, he had run afoul of the law and been rescued from a life in prison by the Children's Aid Society.

"So?" Hush asked. "I never seen the Queen of England, but she don't scare me neither."

Hush was a streetwise Bowery boy from New York's notorious flophouse district. Left homeless after cholera swept though his immigrant tenement and killed both parents, he had at first earned his living selling matches and hawking newspapers. Then he had fallen in with a knuck—an experienced thief—and learned to file down skeleton keys. Hush, too, had been plucked from a jail cell and marked out for a life of redemption in Zebulon Pike's Great American Desert.

Esther Buchanan swept her eye over the rest of them. Near the rear of the car all by himself sat little Spider Winslowe. Painfully shy, an habitual loner, he had once seen a ventriloquist perform on a street corner. Since then, all the poor, lonely thing did was play with Mr. Wigglewobble, a straw-stuffed shirt with a hat sewn to it.

Esther was not a sentimental woman; hers was not a job for the softhearted. Nonetheless, she felt her throat pinch shut as she looked at the children, so young, scared, so alone in the hostile and strange new world. There was little Sarah Pettigrew, left on a doorstep at age five when her immigrant parents discovered that the streets of America were lined with the poor and homeless, not with gold. There was Charlie Brace, only a year older. Which family would pick him to live with them?

The orphan trains were a uniquely American invention, combining pragmatism with genuine compassion. Esther knew Hush was right, even though he was always carping. Some of the settlers did indeed abuse the children who were brought out to replace all the young ones lost during infancy and childhood. There was no end of work to do, and more than one child had been held out of school to work from sunup to sunset.

But many other settlers lived up to their agreements with the Children's Aid Society and treated the children as full members of the family. The children would detrain in town after town. Some would be selected right away; others might ride to the very end of the line and return unclaimed. Esther had escorted hundreds of the orphans, but it still tore at her inside each time she said good-bye to one of them.

"Hush," she said in a kinder voice, turning around again. "I didn't mean to snap at you. You're really a good boy. You just need to watch that foul mouth of yours."

"Aw," he said, his own voice softening, "you ain't so bad neither, I don't s'pose."

"Hey! Look up here!" a voice said from the front of the coach. Everyone stared, but no one was there.

"Spider," Esther said, smiling, "that was you, wasn't it?"

The bashful young lad only turned his face toward the window, flushing. But he held his makeshift dummy up. "It was me, not Spider!" a muffled, high-pitched voice said. Little Sarah Pettigrew laughed with delight and clapped her hands together.

Orphan Train

"Shoot!" Hush said. "That was good. I didn't even see your lips move! Do some more!"

The coach suddenly filled with clamoring voices and shouts for more entertainment. But a few heartbeats later, as the train emerged from a long curve between two steep embankments, the entire world exploded and the train was hurled from the tracks.

Chapter Three

It was the way among red men to mark every important transition in life with a gift to those who were important. At the first opportunity after Honey Eater told him he was to become a father, Touch the Sky gathered his loyal band around him in the safety of the common corral.

Indeed, they had been forced to begin meeting there after the murder of Black Elk one winter earlier. With the tribe's ponies surrounding them, they were safe from supposedly accidental bullets and arrows, because everyone knew how Black Elk had once sent a bullet through Touch the Sky's buckskin shirt, claiming he had mistaken his enemy for an elk. Many in the tribe would gladly sully the medicine arrows by killing Touch the Sky and his friends in cold blood.

Orphan Train

Well used to Touch the Sky's summons, none in his band expected their leader to act almost timid and shy, a manner no man associated with the mighty Bear Caller. Yet clearly he was as nervous as a junior warrior about to hang from the pole for his soldier-troop initiation. Little Horse, Tangle Hair, and Two Twists all curiously eyed the fiber morral Touch the Sky carried in one hand.

At first, as was the custom, they shared a pipe and spoke of inconsequential matters. But when Touch the Sky was slow to state the matter close to his heart, Little Horse finally said, "Buck, have you joined the Peyote Soldiers? If you have some trouble to tell us, no need to spare us the bloody news. These two dug babies beside you may plan to grow fat and toothless, but I have no hopes to die in my sleep. What do you have for us?"

"This," Touch the Sky said, reaching into the morral, then handing Little Horse a small object wrapped in a square of soft chamois. "Brother, how well can you picture the face of Henri Lagace?" Though he spoke of a dead white man, Touch the Sky made the cutoff sign out of respect for the supernatural.

Hearing that name, Little Horse paused in the act of unwrapping the object. He nodded solemnly. "How well? I see it as clearly as if it were painted on my eyelids, Cheyenne! An evil face with dead stones for eyes and a deep, raw scar from chin to temple. The face of a white devil who destroys the red man with strong water."

Touch the Sky nodded toward the object in Little Horse's hand. "During our last fight, when I sent him to his death, I took that from him. It was my first real trophy in battle and still my most valuable. Only now it is yours, brother."

Bewildered, Little Horse unwrapped the object to reveal a beautifully made Spanish dagger. Its blade was double-honed, fine-tempered steel, the haft pure silver with an exquisite ruby inlaid.

"The words carved in the silver are Spanish," Touch the Sky said. "Tom Riley told me they mean never use me without honor. I could think of no better man to own this fine weapon or live up to those words."

Little Horse stood gaping, unable to comprehend such a fine weapon could even exist, much less be his. Tangle Hair's jaw, too, slacked open when Touch the Sky reached back into the morral, then handed him an intricately carved bone whistle decorated with bright yellow and green feathers. All three of Touch the Sky's companions immediately recognized the Comanche battle colors.

"This," Touch the Sky said, "is the war whistle used by the Comanche war chief named Iron Eyes. The Comanches think these whistles appeal to the thunder to come to their aid. He blew it right before I sent him over. There is no stronger medicine than the sacred objects of an enemy who was killed in battle. Now, Tangle Hair, I give it to you."

He turned to Two Twists. "And you, young jay! You had only fifteen winters behind you when I first called on you to defend your tribe. Not once have you failed me. Take this hackamore. The pony it belongs to is now yours."

Two Twists shook his head as if clearing his eyes from sleep. The buffalo-hair hackamore, plaited with rawhide, was never seen on any pony but Touch the Sky's sabino, a light red with a white belly. He had captured it in a raid on Crows up north of the Yellowstone after counting coup on the owner.

"Your sabino?" Two Twists said, bewildered. "I consider it a better pony even than your medicine-hat mustang. Indeed, the best in the common corral. Brother, I agree with Little Horse. Have you been eating strong mushrooms?"

"No," Touch the Sky said. "I am giving you three, my best and most loyal brothers, these valuable gifts so that you will forever remember the time when I told you I will soon bounce my child on my knee."

For a long moment no one said anything. The only sounds were the snuffling of the horses and the rhythmic chomping as the animals took off the grass.

"Ipewa," Little Horse finally said softly: the Cheyenne word for good.

No other words were needed. Everyone knew that truly important things were little discussed. But the ear-to-ear smiles that Touch the Sky's friends wore spoke eloquently of their feelings because warriors did not often show feelings in their faces.

"Before you even say it, brother," Tangle Hair said, "this good news stops here unless you take it elsewhere."

"I take it nowhere," Touch the Sky said. "Outside of this little circle are many for whom it will not be good news."

"Look sharp," Little Horse said, glancing behind them toward camp. From long habit, his hand fell to the bone-handled knife in his beaded sheath. "A rider approaches."

"It is Spotted Tail," Two Twists said. Although the man approaching was friend, all four braves were instantly apprehensive. Spotted Tail was the leader of the Bow String soldier society, Tangle Hair's troop. His loyalty to the tall brave had lately made his life a hurting place. By silent agreement, Touch the Sky avoided him as much as possible. His coming there could only mean serious trouble was in the wind.

"Brothers," he said, still sitting his piebald that had red streamers on her tail to mark Spotted Tail's rank as a soldier chief. "I have noticed that Wolf Who Hunts Smiling has been absent from camp these past several sleeps."

Touch the Sky was instantly alert. Indeed, this

was the same fact that had been bothering him. "Not only absent, but when he rode out, he pointed his hackamore toward Wendigo Mountain."

"He is not there now," Spotted Tail said bluntly, lowering his voice and glancing back toward camp nervously. "One of my sentries just rode in from the huge bluff west of the paleface camp called Register Cliffs. He saw Wolf Who Hunts Smiling there."

"Doing what?"

"The same thing as Big Tree and Sis-ki-dee," Spotted Tail said. "They were with him, and all three were huddled over the path used by the iron horse."

Touch the Sky needed to hear no more. It was bad enough that all three of those Indian criminals, traitors to the Red Nation, would huddle together anywhere. That they had gathered near a railroad track could mean only one thing—especially since, as Touch the Sky knew full well, they still possessed explosives from their attack on a munitions train several moons ago.

"Two Twists," he said grimly, "you have the bridle. Now go catch up your new horse. All of you, cut out your ponies and return to camp for your battle rigs. Fly, bucks! I fear our wily wolf has treachery firmly by the tail!"

Fly the four Cheyenne warriors did, taking full advantage of their ponies' long summer of grazing. Register Cliffs was perhaps half-a-morning's ride from the Cheyenne summer camp, bearing southeast toward the wide and muddy Platte. But the headland Spotted Tail had mentioned, a wooded bluff around which curved the rails of the Kansas-Pacific, lay even closer. Pushing their mounts hard and taking short cuts along seldom-used game traces, the four Cheyenne warriors reached the final ridge overlooking the tracks even before Sister Sun had climbed straight overhead.

"Look!" Little Horse shouted as they approached the crest of the ridge. He pointed toward a lazy black column of smoke spiraling high over the valley below.

Nervous fear made Touch the Sky's back sweat cold as he urged his mustang over the ridge and got his first glimpse of the scene below. "Maiyun help us."

The scene was confusing. A jet-black locomotive was turned on its side beside a section of torn-and-mangled tracks. The diamond smokestack still gave off a few faint puffs of steam. Two white men in coveralls and pillow-tick caps, presumably the engineer and fireman, lay sprawled near the wreckage. They had raw, bloody spots where their scalps used to be. Another white man, perhaps a brakeman, lay dead farther down the tracks. The tender had jumped the rails, too. But the remaining two coaches and the caboose had only been blown slightly off the tracks and pushed up against the steep embankment behind them.

"There is Wolf Who Hunts Smiling," Touch the Sky said grimly, "and Sis-ki-dee and Big Tree. But what are they doing?"

A larger group of Comanche and Blackfoot renegades sat their horses a little farther back, as if waiting for a signal from their leaders. Those three approached the train cautiously, heading for the first passenger coach.

"They do not even have weapons drawn," Touch the Sky said, wonder tightening his voice. "Why? I can hear Wolf Who Hunts Smiling shouting toward the car in English, telling the passengers to come out. But why are those three seasoned warriors showing so little fear?"

His question was answered a moment later when several young crying children began filing out of the coach! Unlike his confused companions, Touch the Sky quickly understood everything. The orphan trains had started heading west in the year the white man's winter count called 1854, two years before Touch the Sky had left the paleface world.

"Brothers," he said, his lips forming their grim, determined slit as he pulled his Sharps rifle from its boot. "A serious mistake has been made by our wily enemies. I will tell you more later. For now, know this: That train is filled with children who have no parents. Our enemies mean to ransom them. Sis-ki-dee's and Big Tree's men are waiting to take them up on horseback and return with them to Wendigo Mountain. We must keep the children on that train and our enemies off. May the Holy Ones forgive me for what I am about to do!"

Touch the Sky already had a ball seated behind the loading gate and a charge in the pan. He placed a percussion cap on the nib beneath the hammer. He placed the rifle into his shoulder socket, drew a bead on the ground just in front of the first child—a boy in a battered bowler hat—and took up his trigger slack.

The shot made all three renegades below flinch as a geyser of dirt spat up in front of the boy's feet. And the thoroughly frightened lad bounded back onto the train, driving the others before him.

"Now, bucks," Touch the Sky said grimly through clenched teeth. "You have each always fought like five men. Do so now. We must drive the attackers back before they board that train! If they gain it, those children are dead!"

It mattered not to his band that the children below were whiteskins. Even Indian tribes capable of torturing adults for hours for mere entertainment softened toward children. The warrior code—which Plains Indians of honor never lightly violated—called for compassion, too, not just fighting skill and courage. Children, like the elderly and soft brained, were helpless and had to be protected with a warrior's life.

Orphan Train

Nothing proved what depths of depravity and lawlessness the Renegade Nation had sunk to more than the heinous scene below.

Before the trio of red criminals could orient themselves to the attack, Touch the Sky and his band opened up with everything they had. His rifle empty, Touch the Sky wasted no time reloading. His bow and arrow had one definite advantage over his rifle. It took one minute, reckoning by paleface time, to load and fire a percussion rifle twice. In that same time, an experienced warrior could launch 15 to 20 arrows.

The warrior gripped his buffalo-sinew bow in his left hand, reached behind to his foxskin quiver, and seized a handful of flint-tipped arrows in his right hand. As fast as he could notch the arrows onto his string, he launched them below. Touch the Sky did not worry about accuracy, only the volume of shots.

The air between the four braves and the renegades below suddenly turned deadly as Touch the Sky's companions followed his lead. They could hear their arrows thwacking hard off the side of the coaches, making it impossible for anyone to enter the doors at either end. More arrows rained in on the unholy trio.

Wolf Who Hunts Smiling, Sis-ki-dee and Big Tree scrambled for the cover of bushes and boulders. They were still unsure, in their panic to gain safety, where the attack came from. But the renegades waiting nearby had spotted the Cheyenne braves up above them on the ridge.

"Cover down, brothers!" Touch the Sky shouted grimly. "Here comes the volley!"

Below started a din like an ice floe breaking apart as the braves—perhaps 30 or more of them—opened up with their rifles. Rock dust flew into Touch the Sky's eyes as the lead reached them.

"Now, brothers!" he shouted. "They are grouped tight and in the open. While they are reloading, we will break cover and give them the same treatment with the arrows!"

Each brave grabbing another handful of arrows, they boldly leapt out into the open and set their strings to flying once again. Despite the long distance down to their enemies, the sudden onslaught of arrows had its effect. Several renegades cried in pain and toppled from their mounts. The rest, frightened into a new respect, broke for cover as their leaders had.

But Wolf Who Hunts Smiling and his two companions had covered down and could return fire. Touch the Sky and his companions barely gained cover again.

"Well, Bear Caller," Little Horse said grimly, "you told us we must stop them from boarding the train. Stop them we have. But look. Our quivers are almost empty. We are four against a legion. Our position here in high ground is good. But what use is it if we have nothing to fire at them? My shotgun is useless at this range."

Orphan Train

Touch the Sky nodded, his eyes never once leaving the scene below them. "You have truth firmly by the tail, buck. As you say, we are at a standoff. They have numbers over us. Therefore, we cannot simply fight a defensive battle. We must take the bull by the horns or be gored."

Touch the Sky looked at all of his companions. "We can do nothing from here. And those children may be alone down there. I do not know how, but somehow, someway, I must get on board that train."

Chapter Four

Esther Buchanan had turned around in her seat to say something to Hush Cochran when the world exploded around her. The shuddering snap as the passenger coaches jumped the track threw her hard into the wall of the coach. A burst of pain exploded inside her skull and she blacked out. When her eyes fluttered open again, her head throbbed ominously and children screamed all around her.

The car was steeply tilted against an embankment, making it difficult for Esther, who was well into her middle years, to struggle into an upright position.

"Aw, quit pipin' out your damn eyes," Hush grumbled to the younger children. "It's just a train wreck. Mebbe we hit a buffalo! Ain't never seen no bison. They say the bulls got a chin whisker. They say—"

A man's scream of pain and terror from outside the steeply canted passenger coach made Hush fall silent. Her pulse throbbing in her palms, Esther fought her way through a jumble of valises and carpetbags to the windows on the opposite side of the car.

She stuck her head out just in time to watch a smallpox-scarred savage, brass rings dangling from his ears, kneel with one knee on the engineer's neck. He made a quick cut around the man's scalp, then snapped it off in one powerful tug. The sound as the scalp tore loose—like dozens of bubbles popping—made bile shoot up Esther's throat.

"Sweet heart of God," she whispered, fear slamming into her like a fist.

She pulled her head back in and tried to fight down the welling panic. The children were her responsibility. Esther had devoted her life to charity, and though she was frightened, her responsibility to the little ones calmed her immediately. She recalled her training back in New York City. The Children's Aid Society had prepared her for such emergencies with the few Indians who were genuinely hostile.

The children, she recalled, were probably safe for the time being. They would most likely be ransomed, perhaps even kept and raised as Indians—a fate to which death might be preferable. But as a second scream from outside vividly reminded her, adults were fair game for murder. Nor would the Indians hesitate to kill a woman—after they had raped her.

Esther saw the situation clearly. And with three murderous renegades approaching the train, she had no time to debate. If those Indians found her, they would kill her. And if she died, the children were as good as lost.

"Hush?" she whispered. "Hush! Can you hear me?"

"I hear you," Hush said. "Miz Buchanan, what's goin' on out there?"

"Hush, you must listen to me. You're the oldest. You'll have to look after the others. Hush, we've been attacked by Indians!"

"Injins! Man alive! We best pull foot. They—"

"Hush, listen to me! Don't get the other children any more frightened than they are already. Indians will kill me if they catch me, but you children should be safe if you just obey them. Don't try to resist them. Do as they say. I'm going to try to make it back to Register Cliffs and telegraph for help. Do you understand?"

"Lordy! Injins!"

Esther could waste no more time. The Indians were almost upon them. Summoning up will and strength she didn't even realize she possessed, she somehow fought her way through the confusion of heaped possessions and children and gained the rear door of the coach.

Orphan Train

Praying that the Indians wouldn't see her and gathering her calico skirts around her legs, Esther slipped outside. Keeping close to the shadow of the tilted car, she hurried back along the tracks in the direction of Register Cliffs.

"I know that one," Wolf Who Hunts Smiling said. "He will not wait for darkness. Even now it is too quiet up on that ridge. They are counseling, and the issue of it will be trouble for us."

Big Tree, Sis-ki-dee, and Wolf Who Hunts Smiling had dived into a nearby covert when the deadly assault of arrows rained in on them from above. They were trapped, and their ponies had scattered. Several of their wounded men lay around them, raising piteous wails of pain.

"He is always trouble," Big Tree said grimly. "But he depends too much on luck, and luck cannot last a lifetime unless a man dies young."

"Stout words!" Sis-ki-dee said. "What can a handful of them do? It will take time for the hair faces to learn news of their iron horse and stolen children. Nor will the little soldier chief named Carlson be any threat to us, not when he knows we are laying this crime in front of Woman Face's tipi. And how many arrows can they have left? White Man Runs Him has the high ground, but only look between us and him—an open slope."

Sis-ki-dee flashed his crazy grin. "My contrary warriors have all the parts of the beehive gun. We only need to have them fall back and assemble the gun and train it on that slope."

Despite their irritation at the delay, his two companions exchanged approving glances. The beehive gun was Sis-ki-dee's name for the multiple stingers of their captured Requa gun, stolen from the same munitions train that had supplied their nitro pack. The weapon had 25 light barrels arranged horizontally; it was designed to fire seven volleys a minute for a total of 175 shots.

"We can make that slope a hurting place," Wolf Who Hunts Smiling said. "I know Touch the Sky. He will not ride back to camp for help. He cannot. Such a move would pit the Bull Whips against the Bow Strings, and he would not cause a war in his own camp.

"No, he will come down that slope. He will board that train because he knows the children will soon do something if he does not take charge of them. We have far more weapons than just that beehive gun, bucks! We will be ready for him."

"There is nothing else for it. I am going down there now." Touch the Sky had already reloaded his rifle. He handed it to Little Horse. "There will be no time to use this. It will be of more use up here. I am counting on you three to provide what cover you can."

"Are we hair faces who take orders from one man?" Little Horse asked. "Why is it always you who keeps the best sport for himself?"

"Because," Touch the Sky said in English, "none of you understands what I'm saying right now, do you?"

Their perplexed silence was answer enough. Then a moment later they, too, understood. What good would any of them be among English-speaking children?

"But alone, brother?" Tangle Hair said.

"One man is less target than two, Cheyenne. And all of you will be needed out here. Even if I do make it onto that train, I will be alone with just the children. It will be up to you three to keep the renegades off that train."

"Brother," Little Horse said, "what about Tom Riley?"

"I, too, have thought of him. He is the only friend we have at the soldiertown. But Seth Carlson has managed to play the fox. Their big eagle chief now keeps Tom and his pony soldiers well to the south of us near Shoshone River. That means Carlson will be sent when help finally comes."

Touch the Sky had already quickly explained to his baffled companions about orphans. Although Indians could easily understand that a child's birth parents would be dead, it did not follow that any Indian child could ever be homeless or alone and unwanted. To Indians, every adult in camp was a parent to every child.

"Because these children are alone," Two

Twists said wonderingly, "they do not matter? Touch the Sky, you have taught us that we cannot hate the whiteskin race as a tribe, but only individual whiteskins. I agree there are good whites. I have met Tom and Caleb Riley and proudly call each a friend. But this idea of ignoring children because they have no parents is hard to understand."

"I do not defend it," Touch the Sky said. "I left the white man's world, buck. Never forget that. Have you heard me pine to return to it? But never mind this talk, brothers. Why discuss the various causes of the wind when actions are the only remedy? For now I am indeed about to return to the white man's world. I am going to board that train."

"How?" Little Horse asked. "Those renegades are up to something down there. Sis-ki-dee shouted orders, and some of his men faded back behind that pile of scree beyond the curve. What is your plan?"

"My plan?" Touch the Sky had already handed his Sharp's rifle to Little Horse. He gazed down the exposed slope, feeling the blood come into his face as he steeled himself for action. His speckled black medicine hat mustang pranced beneath him, eager to answer the singing in her own wild blood. "Here is my plan."

Then Touch the Sky dug both knees into his pony's flank and screamed a shrill Cheyenne war cry. His mustang surged down the slope, her hooves flinging up divots of soil.

But Touch the Sky had no idea how much firepower was waiting below. The sharp cracking of rifles, the fast twangs of bow strings, the taunting cries of his enemies—all rose in a din above the steady pounding of the sturdy little pony's hooves. She had been trained to run in a zigzag pattern, deliberately slowing and surging to throw off the enemy's aim.

Bullets fanned past Touch the Sky's head so close that he could hear their angry-hornet sound. He slid low and forward, hugging his pony's neck in the classic defensive riding position invented by Cheyenne warriors. He felt the mustang's muscles rippling beneath him, heard her blowing, and saw the train growing closer and closer.

Then, with a stuttering roar, the Requa battery commenced firing on the slope. The first volley slammed into the slope just in front of the mustang, causing her to rear back in fright. Touch the Sky, through sheer force of will and muscle, gentled her enough to get her running again. After another few volleys, the screaming bullets and exploding dirt continued to terrorize the man and his pony.

An arrow pierced the warrior's kit, another sliced a white-hot line of pain as it grazed his back. Then, abruptly, the train loomed up just before him. Touch the Sky didn't bother halting his pony. Tugging hard on her right rein to turn her and slapping hard on her rump to keep her running, he simply rolled off her back and slammed hard into the ground.

Touch the Sky tucked, rolled, and came up on his feet with bullets nipping at his heels. From the corner of his right eye, he saw his pony racing to safety past the far end of the train. Then, he leapt up the steps and reached for the door of the passenger coach.

After Esther left, Hush Cochran had started to lead the children off the train as he was ordered. But then those gunshots had sent them flying back on board. Ever since, the constant shooting outside had kept him and the rest huddled under the seats, well away from the windows.

Sarah Pettigrew was crying for her mother. Several other of the smaller children were sniveling and crying.

"Aw, quit the waterworks," Hush said in an urgent voice just above a whisper. "I can't hear myself think!"

But in fact Hush was as scared as any of them, and he couldn't really be angry at the little ones. Still, it was unnerving when Sarah, Charlie Brace, and some of the others started wailing even louder.

"Don't cry, kids!" Mr. Wiggle-wobble said suddenly. "Let's sing a song! Let's sing 'Pop goes the Weasel.'"

"Atta boy, Spider," Hush said as the little ones

Orphan Train

settled down and began singing along with the straw-stuffed dummy.

There had been a lull in the shooting outside, and Hush used that break to slip on board the car behind them. That car had been empty since the regular passengers had detrained at Register Cliffs. Hush was making sure none of the other kids had gone back there because he didn't want them to see what he had just seen: the dead brakeman sprawled across a seat, an arrow skewering his neck.

That sight had sent the frightened lad scuttling back to his own car, but not before he grabbed the Colt Navy revolver from the dead man's hand. The weapon was tucked into his waistband, under the floppy tails of his shirt.

After that one lull, pandemonium had broken loose again outside. Above the percussion of individual rifles, Hush had heard a repeated volley from some ear-shattering weapon that struck terror into the kids anew. Above all that, the rhythmic pounding of hooves growing closer down that slope beyond them.

Hush nervously slid the Colt out of his waistband, figuring the Indians were attacking the train. Esther had told him to obey the Indians. But he couldn't trust no damn Injins. Hell, hadn't he read tons of dime novels and shilling shockers? He knew what the Indians were like.

Then, with a resounding smash, the door at the end of the aisle flew open. As bullets chased him

Judd Cole

up the steps, a wild-looking warrior burst into the car! Sarah and the rest of the children screamed.

"Look out!" Hush shouted. Then, moving quickly before the Indian could scalp any of the children, Hush pointed the Colt at him and felt it buck hard in his fist when he jerked the trigger.

Chapter Five

"Northern Cheyennes, you say?"

Col. Garret Peatross frowned at his subordinate. He had the distracted manner of a college professor. He wore heavy burnsides and a mustache; his chin was smooth shaven. Silver hair curled over the collar of his tunic.

"Yes, sir," Seth Carlson said. "The report from Register Cliffs mentioned Indians with black feathers and knee-length winter moccasins. The Cheyennes are the only Indians hereabouts who wear crow feathers. The Sioux wear—"

"I didn't ask for a damned lecture on heathen customs, captain!"

"Sir! You asked—"

"You're out of line, soldier! Stow it."

Peatross rose from his desk and crossed to the

Judd Cole

Mercator projection on the back wall. It showed the vast Wyoming and Montana territories. Colored pins marked tribes by geographical area: the Pawnee to the east; the Comanche, Kiowa, and Southern Cheyenne to the south; the Arapaho and Shoshone to the west; the Mandan, Hidatsa, Assiniboin, Crow, and Blackfeet to the north; and right there in Wyoming, the Northern Cheyenne and their Sioux cousins.

"That's Gray Thunder's group," Peatross said. "We've had no trouble from him lately."

"No, sir," Carlson said. "Gray Thunder has been no trouble. But just as the Southern Cheyenne chiefs cannot control Roman Nose and the Dog Soldiers, Gray Thunder has some upstart renegades on his hands."

"Renegades?" Peatross had lately become engrossed in writing his memoirs. He was grooming himself for a second career in politics when he retired in six months. While he was honest enough and tried to live up to the letter of the various treaties, he had a bad habit of leaving too much to his junior officers. Although he personally disliked Capt. Carlson's obsequious manner, he had become dangerously dependent on the man's knowledge of local Indians.

"Yes, sir. There's a troublemaker. A big, broad-shouldered buck who goes by the name of Touch the Sky. He leads his own band. I'll wager anything they're the ones who attacked this train."

Orphan Train

"At any rate, you'll have to mount a rescue force at once."

"Yes, sir. Sgt. Ryan is mustering my platoon now. Short rations and each man's to take thirty rounds, crimped and ready. We'll be out the front gate in fifteen minutes."

"Yes, well, don't start busting caps until you know where those children are. What is the exact situation at the train?"

"That won't be clear until it's reconnoitered, sir. According to the telegraphed message of the survivor who made it to Register Cliffs, there've been some deaths, evidently the engineer and fireman among others. This was all reported by the matron who got away."

Peatross nodded thoughtfully, gazing at the map again. "By now those children are either dead or taken hostage. Find out what you can. This is all I need right before I retire. If this situation gets fouled up, I could see my pension halved."

Carlson had to bite his lower lip to keep from smiling. Peatross might be sweating, but Carlson felt positively giddy with elation at the golden opportunity to finally give Touch the Sky the comeuppance he so richly deserved. Carlson was a graduate of West Point and a scion of the F.F.V.—the First Families of Virginia. Yet Hiram Steele's daughter Kristen had chosen to love Touch the Sky over him! Carlson brooked hu-

Judd Cole

miliation from no man, least of all a gut-eating savage.

Carlson wasn't foolish enough to trust Wolf Who Hunts Smiling and his insane, murdering allies. But they had involved him in their plot because they shared his intense hatred for Touch the Sky. With the renegades and the cavalry plotting together, the arrogant red bastard would soon be rowed up Salt River for good.

"I wouldn't worry about your pension, Colonel. Those children are orphans—street urchins and criminal trash, at that. Nobody is going to wake snakes over a bunch of kids nobody wants."

Peatross turned from the map and stared at Carlson sharply. "Captain, I'm not one to slop over emotionally. But sometimes you disgust the hell out of me. Whoever those children are, they're still children. Is that clear?"

"Yes, sir!"

"Now rather than standing there belittling them, see what you can do about rescuing them!"

"Sir!"

Carlson took two precise steps backward, saluted smartly, performed an about-face, and left. Outside, Carlson's men cantered through the gate in sets of four, swallow-tail guidon snapping in the breeze, and they broke into a gallop until they were well clear of the towers at Fort Bates. But once out of sight behind the tableland north of the Bighorn River, Carlson slowed his troopers to an easy trot. He dropped back until his

Orphan Train

sorrel was keeping pace with that of a redheaded top sergeant.

"Sgt. Ryan!"

"Sir?"

"Men look a bit thirsty, do they?"

Ryan grinned. The savvy old soldier knew his platoon commander well. "Thirsty? My hand to God, Cap'n, they're dried to jerky!"

Carlson's big, bluff face was left half in shadow by the wide black brim of his officer's hat. One side of the hat was bent smartly back and snapped to the crown. Carlson reached into his panniers and slid out several bottles of good grain mash, handing them to his top sergeant. "Pass these back through the ranks. Compliments of Col. Peatross."

Touch the Sky didn't even have time to leap before the wild-eyed paleface youth shot the Colt pistol at him. Fortunately, the inexperienced youth bucked the weapon when he fired it, jerking the trigger and ruining his aim. The first slug whistled past Touch the Sky's right ear and whacked into the wood paneling behind him.

The littlest children were screaming and crying; the older ones wore faces of sheer panic as they faced the savage bent on scalping all of them. Even as the young marksman fired his second shot, Touch the Sky dropped to the floor, shouting in perfect English, "Tadpole, lower your hammer! I came to help you!"

Judd Cole

A prolonged silence followed the completely unexpected outburst. Quickly Touch the Sky looked up from the floor and added, "We Indians have our criminals, too, just like you white folks. I'm your friend. My name is Touch the Sky, and I'm a Northern Cheyenne. Those Indians who attacked you are renegade criminals. What's your name?"

"Hush, sir. Hush Cochran, Mr. Sky."

Despite the danger of their situation, the young paleface's nervous response prompted a grin from the Cheyenne. As Hush lowered the Colt, Touch the Sky stood up. All the children stared at him as if a pink elephant had just boarded with them.

"Well, Hush, I'm mighty glad you need lessons in shooting. Now I'm going to tell all you kids how it is. But you bigger boys"—Touch the Sky looked at Hush, Tommy Truesdale, and Spider Winslowe—"are going to have to take charge of the rest. Do you understand? Out here in the West, the best man becomes the law."

When Hush and the other two boys swelled up importantly, Touch the Sky said, "Here's the way it is. Those Indian criminals outside plan to steal you kids and hold you for ransom. They believe that all whites are rich and that your parents will pay them well for your return."

"That's a good one! Ain't none of us got no parents," Hush said.

"No," Touch the Sky said. "But you have

friends, and I'm one of them. Believe me, Hush, Indian or no, I know the feeling of not belonging, of not being wanted. When you're alone in the world, you have to fight harder. But that hard fighting can build real character. Now we've got a hard fight on our hands, and we're going to find out what you kids have got in you."

The moment Touch the Sky fell silent, a bullet shattered a window, and the little ones screamed in terror. Keeping his head down, Touch the Sky said, "Listen, kids! I have three friends outside—three of the best friends a man could have, and three of the best fighters in the Cheyenne Nation. They're out there on top of that ridge. They are the only thing keeping those Indian criminals from boarding this train. We have to help my friends. Do you understand? They can't save you all by themselves."

"I understand, sir," Hush said solemnly.

"Me, too," Tommy Truesdale said.

After a long moment, the silent and shy Spider nodded. Touch the Sky noticed the clothed dummy in his lap. "Can that quiet guy hold a weapon?" the Cheyenne asked, grinning and coaxing a smile out of Spider.

"My name is Mr. Wiggle-wobble." the dummy's high-pitched voice said, and Touch the Sky marveled that the boy's lips hadn't even moved!

But the moment of levity was short-lived. Touch the Sky immediately set to work organizing the orphans for whatever defensive stand they could muster.

"Okay, kids, listen up. Rule number one: No one pokes his head above the windows. Got it?"

When the children answered in the affirmative, Touch the Sky said, "Good. Now can anybody tell me if there's anyone in the car behind us?"

"Just a dead man," Hush said solemnly. "That's where I got this pistol."

More shots from outside sent lead thwacking into the car and caused more screams. But so far, the renegades had not risked rushing the train again—not with three determined Cheyenne warriors waiting up above to cut them down. But eventually sheer numbers would win out. Nor, Touch the Sky thought grimly, could anyone afford to match wits with Big Tree and Sis-ki-dee—two specialists in terrorizing their victims.

"All right," he said to Hush. "Was there a cartridge belt?"

Hush nodded, looking sheepish. "I forgot it."

"We'll get it in a minute. But if you're going to pack a short iron, Hush, you'd best have a lesson in using it. First of all, don't waste time aiming it the way you did when you shot at me. You don't need to aim a pistol. You point it, just as if it was a part of your finger, at your target and shoot.

"Next, don't jerk the trigger. Squeeze it slow and steady, taking up the slack. Otherwise you'll buck your gun and miss. Got it?"

Orphan Train

Hush swallowed audibly and nodded again. "Yes, sir, Mr. Sky."

"The name is Touch the Sky, not Mr. Sky. You have my permission to call me by my name because that's the English version of it. The Cheyenne words cannot be pronounced by white men. Indians believe their names lose their magic if pronounced by whites."

That moment was no time for such trivia, Touch the Sky knew. But children were naturally curious, and already his talk was calming them as they became absorbed in listening.

"Gee, Touch the Sky," Tommy Truesdale said, "do Indians—"

Tommy never finished his question. The renegades had silently been readjusting the aim of their Requa gun. The multibarreled weapon stuttered again and again, throwing a virtual wall of lead into the coach.

Shards of glass sprayed the coach and wood splintered. The racket seemed like some spawn of the white man's hell. Even as Touch the Sky hit the floor again, he saw a wave of red marauders sweeping at them from an oblique angle, trying to avoid the defenders on the ridge.

As soon as the Requa battery quit peppering the coach, Touch the Sky sprang to his feet and leapt to one of the shattered windows. From the right flank raced a line of Comanche and Blackfoot renegades; down the slope, his braid flying out in a straight line behind him, Little Horse came with death in his eyes and his four-barreled shotgun at the ready.

What Touch the Sky next witnessed matched anything he had ever seen for heroism and fighting courage and sheer, death-defying combat skill. His courageous Cheyenne brother rode straight into the teeth of bullets and arrows, not even bothering to hold on to his little piebald's reins, bouncing along on top with perilous ease. One after the other, he revolved the barrels of his scattergun, blasting away at full choke and blowing renegade faces into stew meat.

When his shotgun was empty he dropped it into his fringed boot, removed his bone-handle knife, and buried it deep in another renegade's chest. With a half dozen of their brothers slaughtered in the space of a few heartbeats, the charge was broken. Little Horse whirled his pony, gouged her flanks with his heels, and tore back up the slope. Two Twists and Tangle Hair made sure no foolish bucks pursued him.

"Lordy!" said Hush, who had witnessed the attack through a shattered window despite the order to cover down. "Was that a Cheyenne, too?"

"Actually," Touch the Sky said, pride evident in his voice, "what you just witnessed was the equal of five Cheyennes. That was Little Horse, and I trained as a warrior with him."

"He's savage as a meat ax," Hush said.

Despite his pride in his red brother, Touch the Sky knew full well Little Horse didn't have many more rides like that left in him. Nor could he have many more shells left for his shotgun. More charges were coming. So was Mother Night. And once Sister Sun went to her resting place, Big Tree and Sis-ki-dee would be in their murderous element.

Touch the Sky and the children were caught between the sap and the bark. The army might eventually show up, but Touch the Sky expected little help from that quarter. The longer they remained there, the deeper they dug their own graves.

Chapter Six

"You aren't really telling me," Seth Carlson said, "that four braves are holding this operation up?"

"No, hair face," Wolf Who Hunts Smiling said. "Not four braves. Woman Face and his band. Tell us, brave white pony soldier, how many times have you failed to defeat them?"

Carlson had no ready reply. He stood parleying with the three renegades behind a spine of rocks near the train. To avoid trouble should settlers happen by, he had left his men in a sheltered hollow about a mile back down the trail.

"I expected you to have those brats and be smoke by now," Carlson said. He spoke in English, which was understood well by Wolf Who Hunts Smiling and the Comanche Big Tree. Siski-dee, too could follow the jist of his remarks.

Orphan Train

Carlson pointed toward the bodies near the front of the train. "Look at the situation from my point of view. Not only have you kidnapped white children. You've murdered whites! I can't drag my damned feet forever. Either you get those damn kids and skedaddle, or I'm going to have to rescue them."

"No, blue blouse," Wolf Who Hunts Smiling said. "We did not kill palefaces and steal children. White Man Runs Him did this thing, along with his band. Have you already forgotten how that is the reason for all this trouble?"

Carlson nodded, taking the warrior's meaning well. The savage was right—the golden opportunity to focus the wrath of a white nation on his worst enemy in the world was at hand. Never mind that these savages were in for a rude surprise when no whites would offer a ransom for the orphans. Carlson figured it was no skin off his nose.

"I haven't forgotten," Carlson said. "But how much longer are you going to be?"

"With that one? You know better than to ask. But we can defeat him and his band. There can be little food and water on that train. His band will eventually run out of bullets and arrows. With time we can easily defeat them."

"Time? That's the one thing I don't have. My C.O. expects action. My men should already have engaged yours by now."

"Suppose," Big Tree said, "that your men were

suddenly called back to the soldiertown? Suppose wild Indians attacked settlers near Fort Bates?"

Carlson was about to object. Then he realized the plan just might work. Fort Bates was currently understaffed with veteran troops, having recently become a recruit garrison for basic training. Carlson's Indian-fighting platoon was the only unit currently up to operational strength. No matter how important rescuing those orphans might be to Col. Peatross, his first obligation was to protect the settlers who lived there.

Carlson nodded. "That might work. But it would have to be quick."

"It will be." Wolf Who Hunts Smiling grinned at his two Indian companions. "Pick a few of your best riders. Send them down to Bighorn Falls. Have them kill a settler or two and start enough fires to stir the hair faces to a panic. Not much will be needed. They are ready for the warpath if we even steal a cow."

Sis-ki-dee had said nothing during their exchange. All of a sudden he threw his head back and roared with insane laughter. "We cooperate now, hair face. I confess I like your treachery! But once we have sent this Touch the Sky to sleep with the worms, I plan to string my next bow with your guts!"

* * *

Orphan Train

"Count upon it, Aunt," Honey Eater said to Sharp Nosed Woman. "My husband spoke straight when he said that Wolf Who Hunts Smiling has cleaned his parfleche of honor and filled it instead with ambition. Look at him over there, plotting even now with that skinny bone-blower! Where is Touch the Sky? Where are Little Horse and Two Twists and Tangle Hair? They have been gone too long. Some terrible new trouble is afoot."

"Indeed, niece," her aunt said. "Lately, trouble is the ridge this tribe has camped upon."

The two women sat before Sharp Nosed Woman's tipi, shelling wild peas into a bowl. Wolf Who Hunts Smiling had just returned to camp. He had immediately crossed to the tipi of the so-called shaman Medicine Flute. For some time those two had sat with their heads close. Honey Eater knew her world was about to become a hurting place once again.

Now and then Medicine Flute cast a glance across the camp clearing in her direction. He had already informed Honey Eater, lust constricting his voice, that he planned to take her as his woman once her husband was sent under and Wolf Who Hunts Smiling led the tribe. She thought of his heavy-lidded eyes, soft, girlish skin, and high-pitched voice that cracked like an adolescent's. A shiver of disgust coursed through her.

But there was no more time for such unpleasant thoughts. Suddenly Wolf Who Hunts Smiling called the camp crier to his side. Moments later his pony was racing up and down the camp paths as he called all the people into the common clearing.

"Now," Honey Eater said bitterly as her aunt and she joined the people streaming into the clearing, "the wily wolf will speak in a bark. And look, Aunt. See how the soldiers have all come into the clearing with their battle rigs?"

Sharp Nosed Woman nodded, her careworn face saddened at the outrageous barbarity. "The heathen Comanche kill each other in their own camps. We have descended to their level. How much longer can the bloodshed be avoided?"

"Time is a bird," Honey Eater said, quoting old Arrow Keeper, "and the bird is on the wing. The battle is coming. But I pray to Maiyun that the traitors will not make their move tonight while Touch the Sky and his band are gone. I do not think Spotted Tails's Bow String troopers, loyal though they are, can stop these murderous Bull Whips!"

She fell silent as they reached the throng gathered before the hide-covered council lodge at the center of camp. Wolf Who Hunts Smiling, short in stature though wiry, fast, and strong, had leapt onto a cottonwood stump. His lupine features were eerily traced in the orange flames of a huge clan fire.

Orphan Train

"Fathers! Brothers! Cheyenne people! Have ears for my words!"

"Why?" Spotted Tail shouted out boldly. "You are neither a peace chief nor a war leader. You do not head a soldier troop or a clan. By which of our ancient law ways do you claim the right to send out the crier and assemble the people?"

"By this law way, you milk-livered licker of white men's feet!" Wolf Who Hunts Smiling roared back, unsheathing his knife and brandishing its lethally honed blade in the firelight. "Interrupt me one more time, and I will open you up from rump to throat in front of your filthy squaw!"

Those shocking words made Honey Eater suddenly feel faint with fear. Spotted Tail was one of the most respected warriors in camp, a troop leader! To insult his good wife for no reason could only mean that the Whips were spoiling for a battle. But Spotted Tail sent a high sign to his troopers, restraining them.

Wolf Who Hunts Smiling continued. "Cheyenne people! Place my words in your sashes. They are words of substance that you may pick up and examine. We know, from reports of our scouts, that Big Tree's Comanches and Sis-ki-dee's Blackfoot warriors have made common cause and established their camp atop Wendigo Mountain. Nothing could be more dangerous for our tribe than these two marauders so close to hand! We Bull Whips have kept a vigilant eye on them. Although we cannot attack them on such high, formidable ground, we can protect our camp from any attack."

"Honey Eater!" Sharp Nosed Woman said, grabbing her niece and pulling her back when she suddenly surged forward to protest his hypocrisy. "They will kill you here and now!"

But the worst was to come. His eyes watching for the attack, Wolf Who Hunts Smiling said, "Fathers! Brothers! Can anyone explain why we have seen Touch the Sky and his followers journeying so often to Wendigo Mountain? Or why they always come back safe? Where is White Man Runs Him and his band now, as I speak? Does their absence have the sanction of council on it?

"No! Once again they have mysteriously disappeared. Medicine Flute! Step forward and share with your tribe the vision you reported to me."

Honey Eater felt her stomach roiling in disgust when the slender-limbed brave clumsily mounted the stump. He almost fell off because his balance was so bad. As always, he clutched a flute made from a human leg bone. He claimed that its monotonous notes granted him strong medicine.

Honey Eater had noticed how adept Medicine Flute was at playing on the Cheyenne people's often naive belief in visions. Realizing that men known as vision seekers never had to hunt or fight, the crafty coward had perfected a certain trance state that impressed many of the people. He did so then, putting a glaze over his eyes and speaking in an odd voice that did not seem to emanate from him.

"There is music in the spheres, destiny in a handful of sand. Those who claim to see visions are many, but few ever tread the upward path of the spirit way. Fewer still produce true acts of strong medicine. Any fool can clap his hands at the moment a tree begins to fall down, then claim he clapped that tree down. This is how the woman-faced Touch the Sky performs medicine.

"But who among you will promise well ahead of the event to set the largest star in the heavens on fire and then trail it, burning, across the sky? I did this thing!"

Honey Eater seethed with rage, and only her aunt's restraining hand kept her back. Touch the Sky had explained the burning-star miracle. It was called a comet, and Medicine Flute knew it was passing over because the white man's science predicted its coming. But many of the people had fallen down in hysteria, claiming Medicine Flute was truly a great shaman.

"Now," Medicine Flute said, "another important vision has been placed over my eyes by Maiyun, the Day Maker. In this vision, I saw the Cheyenne people afloat atop a roaring river of blood! I saw our ponies throats slashed, our babes slammed against trees, our women topped

Judd Cole

by bluecoat pony soldiers, and our warriors made weak and unmanly from strong water. In short, I saw the entire Cheyenne nation on its own funeral scaffold. And I saw Touch the Sky sitting on a hill with his hair-face friends, laughing at our suffering!"

"Cheyenne people!" Wolf Who Hunts Smiling shouted, pulling his lackey down and leaping back up on the stump. "Do you have ears? Do you comprehend? Even now, Touch the Sky plays the fox against his tribe, conspiring in some new mischief with these cricket-eating renegades. Count upon it! The issue of his treachery will be the destruction of this tribe!"

A collective roar of protest went up from the Bull Whips. Lone Bear, leader of the Whips, spoke. And when he did, Honey Eater realized that her worst fear was true: The Whips planned to move that very night!

"Fathers! Brothers! Have you forgotten that this Touch the Sky must surely have murdered he who may not be mentioned—the best war leader this tribe ever had and my best soldier? And now he ruts on that good man's widow. Whips! Will we continue to tolerate this pretend Cheyenne's supporters in our very camp? Or will we move this very night to place true Cheyennes in power?"

The Bull Whips roared as one man, many of them brandishing their weapons.

"Bow Strings!" Spotted Tail shouted. "If you

love truth and honor, prepare to die for them. The fight has come to us!"

Fear had formed a ball of ice in Honey Eater's stomach. Crying out, many of the women had grabbed children and started to herd them out of harm's way. The two factions were already squaring off for the bloody clash. Abruptly, a powerful shout claimed everyone's attention.

"Hold! I command it in the name of these!"

Honey Eater joined everyone else present in turning to stare toward a lone tipi on a hummock between the clearing and the river. Chief Gray Thunder stood just outside his entrance flap, clearly visible in the flickering firelight. Although well past his fortieth year, he was still a vigorous warrior whose battle exploits commanded respect.

But it wasn't his coup feathers that instantly claimed everyone's rapt attention. In his right hand, Gray Thunder held a knife to his own throat; in his left, he held the tribe's sacred medicine arrows! Only two people in the tribe knew where those Arrows had been hidden: Touch the Sky, who as shaman was also the Arrow Keeper, and Gray Thunder, who had a right to know as peace leader.

Those four arrows—shafts painted in blue and yellow stripes, tipped with flaked flint, fletched with bright red feathers—symbolized the fate of the entire tribe. It was believed that the arrows must be kept forever clean. Whatever befell the arrows would befall the tribe.

"It has come to this sad thing," Gray Thunder said. "And now I say this. The first act of violence by any warrior in this camp will not only kill your peace chief, but leave his blood on the sacred arrows! Now go on, young hotheads! Destroy your people!"

Honey Eater knew his threat was a desperate but brilliant move. Already the warriors were standing down, sheathing their weapons. Very few among them were irreverent enough to risk bloodying the arrows.

Looking keenly disappointed, Wolf Who Hunts Smiling nonetheless gave up. Gray Thunder was too well respected to force the issue. But the triumph gleaming in Medicine Flute's eyes, as he again gazed across toward Honey Eater, made a cool feather of fear tickle the bumps of her spine.

The clan fires were still burning when the three Cheyennes met in Medicine Flute's tipi.

"You are sure of this thing, cousin?" Wolf Who Hunts Smiling said.

The young woman named Grasshopper, a member of Wolf Who Hunts Smiling's Panther Clan, nodded.

"I swear it, cousin. Honey Eater still reports to the Once-a-month lodge with the rest of us, as we Cheyenne women must when our bleeding time comes. But I tell you, she is not bleeding!

Orphan Train

She is trying to fool us. But count upon it. A child grows inside her."

At that news, the two braves exchanged long, troubled looks.

"That is not just a child inside her," Medicine Flute said. "It is his child! Do you take my meaning?"

"What? Do you take me for a soft brain?" Wolf Who Hunts Smiling snapped irritably. "Of course I take your meaning."

The wily brave looked perplexed. "I do not understand. Everyone said Honey Eater's womb was barren. My cousin"—he made the cutoff sign for speaking of the dead—"was as virile and strapping a buck as I have ever seen. Yet he could not sire a whelp with her."

"This child must not be born!" Medicine Flute said. "This is a sign, a warning! Grasshopper here is a shy young thing. No one told her to come to us with this news. Yet she did. We are being warned! Act like men now, or delay longer and die like white-livered Poncas!"

Although he despised Medicine Flute for his cowardice, Wolf Who Hunts Smiling never doubted his intelligence. Nor did he really need convincing. The very idea of allowing Touch the Sky's child—especially a son—to enter this world was preposterous. It was proving task enough to kill the father. Wolf Who Hunts Smiling did not want to go through the struggle again to kill the son.

"Think about it," Wolf Who Hunts Smiling said. "This Woman Face is close to death now. Who knows? When we return to the iron horse, perhaps we will learn that Sis-ki-dee and Big Tree have already killed him. True words?"

Medicine Flute had just inserted his flute into his lips. But he pulled it back out since his companion's shrewd grin foretold more merry sport. "True words."

"Good. And what would a woman who loves as deeply as Honey Eater loves her brave do when her man dies? Why, buck! She would march backward off the cliffs of the Wolf Mountains, singing a song of his praises as she fell to her own death! At the very least, she would take his best knife and fall on it herself."

Medicine Flute nodded slowly, his lazy, drooping eyelids making him look sinister and unholy in the light from the firepit. "And if she does not fall on it, we will throw her on it."

Chapter Seven

"I see no reason," Sis-ki-dee said to Big Tree, "why we should not have a bit of sport."

With Several of the braves already on their way south to attack Bighorn Falls, the threat of bluecoat intervention was removed for the moment. Wolf Who Hunts Smiling had returned to his tribe to plant seeds of destruction against the tall Bear Caller who could summon the grizzly to his side. The two renegades rested comfortably in the lee of the same bank against that which the train coaches were tilted.

Big Tree took one more puff from the long clay calumet, grimacing at the somewhat bitter taste of the leaf-and-bark kinnikinnick. He missed the rich white man's tobacco. But soon, the ransom for these pale whelps would buy many fine things.

"Sis-ki-dee," he said, "I once believed there was no Indian from where we sit now to the place where the sun goes down who could match me for treachery. I was wrong twice. Once was with Wolf Who Hunts Smiling. Twice was with you! If you have sport in your thoughts, do not play the coy woman. Speak words I can carry."

Sis-ki-dee liked that reply. At the very moment he had been born, claimed the old grandmothers of his tribe, a wild-eyed black stallion had raced past the tipi. And true to the awful omen, he had grown up wild-eyed and crazy dangerous.

"Someday, Big Tree," he said, nodding, "one of us will kill the other. You know that, do you not?"

Big Tree grinned, the furrow between his eyes deepening. "Of course I know that. But for now, let us join forces for mutual profit. What manner of sport do you mean?"

At that moment a geyser of dirt shot out of the bank near Sis-ki-dee's head; an eyeblink later the sound of the rifle reached them. The brave dove for better cover.

Big Tree laughed so hard he was forced to hawk up phlegm before he could speak. "Do you take my meaning now? Either we cooperate, or we will never have our chance to kill each other. These Cheyenne are sworn to take our last breath from our nostrils."

After his first surprise passed, Sis-ki-dee, too,

Orphan Train

roared with laughter. "Good shooting, warriors! When I top your mother, I will compliment you!"

"Truly?" one of them shouted back. "When I top yours, I will wipe the dirt from my moccasins since you were spawned from mud!"

Anger flickered in Sis-ki-dee's eyes, and seeing it, Big Tree roared again. "Look! Even the brainer of babies shows his feelings when these Cheyennes bait him."

"Will you rattle on like some doting squaw?" Sis-ki-dee said. "You and Wolf Who Hunts Smiling both! All this useless mouth wind about your hatred for Touch the Sky. Are you ready to have some fine sport before we kill him?"

"Is a fit buck ready to rut?"

"Tell me," Sis-ki-dee said. "Who is the finest horseman, red or white, on the high plains?"

He staggered back against the bank hard when the huge Comanche thumped him hard in the chest with his open hand.

"Buck, the finest horseman just struck you," Big Tree said.

Sis-ki-dee nodded, pulling himself back up to his feet. "And who is unsurpassed in the art of stealth and silent movement? In the art of driving his victims to a frenzy of terror?"

Again Sis-ki-dee thumped into the embankment when Big Tree struck his chest. "Buck, I just struck that warrior."

"Straight words. And if you strike him again,

your name ceases to be spoken. But have you caught my drift yet?"

Big Tree nodded. "I will attack the iron horse, send a few bullets inside, and make as if to board. But it will all be a feint."

"Your thoughts fly with mine. While you distract the tall one and his fanatical followers on that ridge, I will sneak aboard through the last car, the one that looks like a lodge on wheels. The Cheyenne will not expect this attack in daylight. When Sister Sun goes to her rest, the night will belong to blood and Sis-ki-dee!"

More than ever, Touch the Sky needed to rely on the Warrior Way taught to him by Arrow Keeper. It had been ominously quiet except for an occasional shot or two from the ridge as his vigilant friends above kept Sis-ki-dee and Big Tree scrambling for cover. Touch the Sky knew his friends could send one of their number—Tangle Hair, who was the swiftest rider—racing back to camp for more ammunition and badly needed supplies. But that would leave only two to hold that ridge against a possible massed attack on the train.

The children, at least, had quieted although occasionally one of the littlest ones loosed a sniffle or a whimper. The older orphans, even Hush, were surprisingly gentle with the younger ones. They reminded Touch the Sky that whites, too, cooperated and cared for each other when hard

Orphan Train

times hit. At least, before they got old enough to get greedy, mean, and ambitious, before they learned to mistrust and hate each other. Touch the Sky himself had been raised among the whites and had never done a white man a wrong. Yet they had turned on him like rabid dogs. Would any of them care for the abandoned children?

Spider had performed a little show with Mr. Wiggle-Wobble, quietly throwing his voice and singing nursery rhymes. Hush, taking care not to expose himself for long, had nonetheless begun to keep a vigilant eye out the various windows. Touch the Sky encouraged him with nods. If they were to survive the death trap, the older boys would have to stand in for men.

Touch the Sky knew that Sis-ki-dee and Big Tree would not waste the approaching darkness. He had also seen the conference with Seth Carlson so he knew the army was cooperating with the Renegade Nation. Even so, the renegades would move quickly. There were disgruntled white miners in the area, vigilantes, the Citizens Militia. They would move against the Indians if they dwelled too long in the valley. Perhaps when Wolf Who Hunts Smiling returned, perhaps before—then the renegades would go for the death blow.

Thinking of Wolf Who Hunts Smiling made the bitter bile of hatred erupt up in Touch the Sky's throat. He could imagine the flames of hatred being fanned back in the camp—the camp where danger lived, where Honey Eater and their unborn child lived.

But the battle-hardened warrior banned such soft thoughts from his mind. Instead, he cleared his head completely, attending only to the language of his senses. He listened for sounds that didn't belong to the train or to nature. But as his sister the sun arced lower in the west, he heard only the familiar river-valley sounds from outside: the harsh calls of grebes and willets, the more melodious notes of the thrushes and larks nesting down near the water.

The peaceful stillness bothered him, as did his shaman sense—the tingling numbness in his scalp. Arrow Keeper had taught him to recognize his shaman sense and, even more, to trust it. That sense drifted back to him, the sere, ailing, yet still vital voice of his old mentor: *For every battle road, there is a spirit road.*

Touch the Sky moved slowly, carefully, up and down the length of the train. The cars in front were too badly mangled to enter. But the car he was in, the car behind it, and the caboose sat upright enough to permit entry—though passing from car to car exposed him to enemy fire.

He did so twice, encountering no resistance either time. His heart hammering against his ribs, but his senses focused and alert, he searched both cars. They were empty for the time being. But again the brave felt the cold, numb

Orphan Train

prickling like a limb falling asleep, crawling up his nape and into his scalp.

He caught Hush Cochran's eye as he returned to the occupied car. "See anything?"

Hush pushed his bowler back with one hand, the one holding the pistol, and wiped sweat from his brow. He shook his head. "Just rocks and trees out the one side and dirt out the other."

"That dirt is saving our lives, boy. That's one flank we don't have to defend."

"Touch the Sky, them bodies outside? Didja see a woman among 'em?" When the Cheyenne shook his head, Hush said, "Maybe Miz Buchanan pulled foot outta here after all! I sure hope so. She was with us. She told me she'd try to make it to Register Cliffs and get help."

Touch the Sky only nodded, not wanting to shatter the scared kid's sole hope. The help had been sent in the form of Seth Carlson. And that white man's hatred for one Cheyenne had put all these children in mortal danger.

Suddenly, dozing children screamed themselves awake at the burst of a rattling, hammering explosion. What glass remained blasted loose in deadly shards. Touch the Sky dropped, then swore in English as he leapt to his feet again to pull the frozen Hush down onto the floor with him.

The Requa battery had started again. More rounds splatted in from the individual rifles of the renegades. But only one horse approached the train, its hoofbeats pounding out a fast drumroll. One horse, one rider, and none more likely to make it than the Comanche trick rider Big Tree!

Touch the Sky snatched the gun from Hush and leapt to his feet as bullets parted his hair. Sure enough, there was Big Tree, a murderous red juggernaut bearing down on them.

Even as he defied death, Touch the Sky knew something was wrong. But he had no time to ponder motives while that superb Comanche pony, a roan as fleet as a white man's thoroughbred yet as strong as a mountain mustang, brought the red killer nearer.

The brave's only thought was to stop the biggest target, the pony, then to worry about the rider. But once again the frustrated Cheyenne realized that, when it came to a Comanche horse and rider, there was no separating one from the other.

Again the Requa stuttered, rounds hammered into the coach, and hysterical children screamed loud enough to wake snakes. Outside, Big Tree's marvelous pony leapt first right, then left, bucked, yet, somehow kept coming forward. Touch the Sky's band, too, were frustrated, finding the mount too difficult to aim for a good shot. And like their Sioux cousins, Cheyennes were bullet hoarders who followed one motto: one bullet, one enemy.

Closer, Touch the Sky urged, just a little closer!

Orphan Train

He knew the pistol was useless beyond perhaps 40 yards, even less with a moving target such as the clever pony.

Window glass pierced his cheek, yet he stood his post, wondering what was the reason for the attack. Did Big Tree mean to board the train by himself in broad daylight? It hardly seemed likely, even for that bold warrior who would steal meat from the Wendigo.

Big Tree hurtled forward. Touch the Sky tasted the salt tang where his injured cheek poured blood into his mouth. He flinched away as more glass sprayed him.

Big Tree pounded closer, relentlessly closer, and Touch the Sky lay his left forearm on the sill of the shattered window. He lay the Colt's long muzzle over it, not to aim the weapon, but to steady it against bucking. His finger slipped inside the trigger guard and began to take up the slack.

Abruptly, as if he knew the very rock where he entered the kill zone, Big Tree reined in his roan. He had reached a spot where neither those on the train nor those on the ridge could easily tap him with a bullet. "Woman Face! Did you enjoy that show?"

"Truly, it was diverting, Quohada!"

"Truly? So was it diverting when I held your honey-skinned wife prisoner down in the Blanco Canyon. When I and my braves topped her and made her cry out in delight at finally tasting men instead of Cheyenne bucks. She had never seen such size on a man."

None of those insults touched the tall Cheyenne. Not only because he was used to them, but because his nagging suspicion had become a certainty. Big Tree was diverting them, all right. But not from boredom. He was diverting them from something more dangerous. And nothing—not the deadly mountain fever, nor the white man's chattering Gatlings—was more dangerous than Sis-ki-dee.

Even as Big Tree whirled his mount and streaked off, his mocking laughter audible, Touch the Sky glanced back toward the end of the train. Outside, Sister Sun sank toward her bed in the west while Touch the Sky again felt the cold, numb prickling on the back of his neck.

Corey Robinson drove in the day's last nail, then wiped the sweat off his forehead as he stepped back to proudly display his work.

Corey was a carpenter, and he had just finished his first major job: building an addition onto the Hotel Wyandot. The hotel, like everything else in Bighorn Falls those days, was booming thanks to the progress on the railroads. New railheads and spur lines meant that stockmen could ship herds off instead of making the long drives to the slaughterhouses in Denver. As a result, more commerce was coming to the Wyoming Territory.

Orphan Train

Corey was well satisfied with his work so far. Each day he had plugged away. But the new pine addition was shaping up nicely. If the hotel owner liked the job Corey did, there'd be plenty more work on the new Stockmen's Association building.

"Good day, Corey Robinson! How are you, lad?"

Corey turned around to confront one of the town's earliest residents, Holly Miller, a seamstress who did outwork for a living. Quickly the young redhead grabbed his cap off his head.

"Howdy, Miz Miller. I'm a mite tired, ma'am, but doing just fine. Thank you."

Corey tried not to gape in open astonishment. Although wide hoop skirts were all the rage back in the East, fashion was slow to arrive on the frontier. But Holly was proudly wearing the first such skirt he had seen in Bighorn Falls. The whalebone crinoline beneath the skirt extended it to a full 18 feet in circumference!

"Well?" she asked. "What do you think?"

Corey hung fire. Being honest with a woman, when it came to telling her how she looked, could land a man in a world of hurt. Yet those damned hoop skirts were complete foolishness, Corey thought. Why, just last week a woman in Denver had burned to death when a spark from a cigar had landed on her voluminous skirts. Another woman in St. Joe had been dragged to her death when her skirts had gotten caught in the door of a runaway carriage.

"Well, you want the truth, ma'am?"

"Yes, Corey Robinson, I most certainly do!"

Corey winked. "You look ravishing. If I could get close enough to you, I'd slip you a kiss."

"Why, you young scoundrel!" But Holly flushed with naughty pleasure. "If your pa wasn't a preacher, I'd—"

Suddenly, an arrow streaked between Holly and Corey and chunked hard into the new wood of a support beam. It struck so hard it cleared the thick beam and dropped out the other side.

More arrows flew in even as Corey grabbed the screaming woman and pulled her to cover behind a partially finished wall. The air was alive with savage war cries and the panicked shouts and screams of the pedestrians thronging Main Street. Unshod-hooves pounded everywhere as gunshots rang out. Then, peering cautiously around a corner of the wall, Corey spotted marauding Indians.

The warriors raced down the wagon-rutted street, scattering townspeople like water before the prow of a ship. Corey's boyhood friendship with Touch the Sky had made him more curious than most settlers about Indians. Thus, he instantly recognized one of the tribes represented in this group: the dreaded Comanches, the Red Raiders of the Plains.

But Bighorn Falls was not in Comanche coun-

Orphan Train

try. Those Indians lived well to the south in the Texas and New Mexico wastelands. One band, however, did come that far north and Corey had helped Matthew fight them: the murdering thieves who rode with Big Tree.

Corey did not see Big Tree in the bunch that was terrorizing his town. Nor could he immediately recognize the other braves, the ones with their hair cut raggedly short. But he knew that Big Tree had thrown in with Blackfoot renegades under the killer Sis-ki-dee.

Even as Corey tried to calm Holly, something else troubled him. The attack was nothing like a typical Indian attack. It was more like the way cowboys behaved when they rode into a town at the end of a hard drive. The renegades were not worried about killing anyone or stealing anything, only in frightening the citizenry. No Indian tribe would bother to enter a white man's town, then ignore all the tempting booty—unless the attack was meant to deliberately stir up trouble. If that was so, then they were likely covering up for something.

"Oh, my stars and garters they'll kill us all!" Holly screamed. "Help! Help!"

"Now shush!" Corey said "You're all right. See. There they go out the other end of town."

But Corey knew everything wasn't all right, not by a long shot. It had been some time since he had heard from his old friend Touch the Sky. The brave would have to be informed of the attack today. What if Big Tree had returned in a second effort to kill the Hanchons, Touch the Sky's adopted parents?

Corey made up his mind. He would ride out to Fort Bates tomorrow and see if Tom Riley was back in garrison. Clearly there was some serious new trouble in the wind.

Chapter Eight

Darkness descended over the stranded train like an indigo cloak, bringing the ominous silence of a secret burial forest with it. Touch the Sky knew he had a long vigil ahead. And he also knew that the safest time to grab some rest before darkness settled in completely was at hand. Accustomed, as were all in his band, to finding sleep in short snatches, he had instructed Hush to be especially vigilant and to wake him at any suspicious sight or sound. Then the weary Cheyenne joined the children on the floor because the seats were too dangerously exposed to fire. He curled up for a few moments rest.

A fitful sleep did come. But so did dream images from his past, sprung from his memory like wild ponies from a corral. Touch the Sky glimpsed the unshaven, long-jawed face of Hiram Steele's wrangler Boone Wilson. He again saw Wilson unsheathing his Bowie knife while Steele's daughter Kristen screamed. Suddenly, the dozing Cheyenne saw the smug, overbearing sneer of Seth Carlson, the bluecoat officer who had helped Steele destroy the Hanchons' mercantile business.

More images flew past like quick geese in a storm. Touch the Sky saw his own people torturing him over fire; the white whiskey trader again slaughtering white trappers and making the killings look Indian; himself counting coup on Seth Carlson when the officer tried to torch the Hanchon spread; the terrified Pawness fleeing from Medicine Lake when he summoned a ferocious grizzly; the keelboat called the *Sioux Princess* exploding into splinters as Touch the Sky led his people to victory over the land grabber Wes Munro during the Tongue River Battle.

Mixed in with all the fragments from the brave's past were glimpses from his vision quest at Medicine Lake, glances stolen from the future. He saw his people freezing far to the north in the Land of the Grandmother and Cheyenne blood staining the snow. The screams of the dying ponies were even more hideous than the death cries of the Cheyenne. His dream led to one huge battle. Then the warrior leading the entire Cheyenne nation in its last great stand turned to utter the war cry, and Touch the Sky recognized the face

Orphan Train

under the long war bonnet as his own.

But another grinning face—an ugly, ferocious, smallpox-scarred face—took over. Then Touch the Sky heard old Arrow Keeper's warning: *Never mind the future, buck! Wake to the living world, or sing your death song*!

The young Cheyenne started violently awake, fear lancing into him. Cold sweat poured from his face, and for a moment in the new darkness, he forgot where he was. Then he remembered.

Darkness had fully arrived, but a full moon sent plenty of ghostly, silver-white illumination through the shattered and bullet-pocked windows. Touch the Sky saw Hush dutifully at his post, prowling up and down the aisle of the coach with the pistol in his hand. Children were scattered everywhere, many having cried themselves to sleep. The two other older boys, Tommy Truesdale and Spider Winslowe, were also awake and vigilant.

"You fellows are doing good work," Touch the Sky said. "Tommy, you and Spider rest now. You'll have to take turns relieving Hush later."

Touch the Sky glanced outside, where moonlight covered the landscape. The renegades were nowhere in sight. Although the warrior couldn't see them, he knew his trusty band were out there, watching, waiting for the ever expected attack. Again he glanced toward the end of the train.

"You hear somethin' back there, Touch the Sky?" Hush asked.

The Cheyenne shook his head. "Not with my ears, but I have a hunch I best take a look back there."

Hush wrinkled his brow in confusion. "Not with your ears? What else could you hear with?"

"If you want to know if it's going to storm hard, you watch the leaves on the trees. When they turn their white sides out, bad weather's on the way. If you want to know if it's going to be a wet or dry summer, you check a spider's web. If it's spun thin, a dry summer is ahead. If it's thick, look for a wet one. You can tell a lot of things without your ears. But for now, just keep yours wide open. How much food do you kids have on board?"

At the mention of food, Hush looked wistful. "Food? Man alive, I could eat boot leather. A few of the kids have a piece of fruit or such, but no more. The locals lay out a big spread for us at each stop. Then, while we're stuffin' our gobs, they walk around among us and pick out the ones they want to live with 'em. I didn't cotton to none that looked at me; so I gave 'em all the rough side of my tongue. You should hear me cuss! I—"

Touch the Sky hushed the boy by placing one hand on his shoulder. "You've brought some bad habits from the white man's world with you to the frontier, little brother. If you want to survive out here, learn to keep your mouth shut when there's trouble in the wind. White men like to pass the time talking. That's when they get killed. Stay quiet and attend only to the language of your senses."

"What senses?"

"Just live up to your name and hush! Stop all the thoughts in your head. Thoughts are just silent words that will distract you as surely as speaking. Be awake and aware, and you will learn to use your senses."

It was time for Touch the Sky to follow his own advice. The coach and caboose behind them would have to be searched, and they would have to be searched throughout the night.

Again he thought about that suspicious charge Big Tree had made, creating more smoke than fire. And he saw Sis-ki-dee's grinning face that had wakened him from sleep just moments earlier.

Touch the Sky drew a deep breath to fortify himself. Then, with one hand resting on the beaded sheath of his knife, he headed toward the back of the coach.

"Well I'll be," Capt. Tom Riley said softly. "That explains it."

"Explains what?" Corey Robinson said.

"These."

Tom whacked the deal table in front of him with the knuckles of his right hand. A sheaf of papers lay there, the official seal of the U.S. War Department across the top of the first page.

"TAD orders, Temporary Additional Duty. Means I keep my usual job as a platoon commander of cavalry. But temporarily I have a new assignment. Assistant to the quartermaster. A damned coffee-cooler job for the slackers in Company Q. Who wouldn't be a soldier?"

"I'll bet a blue banjo it was Seth Carlson behind it," Corey said.

Tom nodded glumly. He was a sunburned towhead in his twenties; the top of his brow was as white as moonstone where his hat protected it. He had been on extended patrol down south of the Smoky Hill River. Those orders had been waiting the moment he had returned that morning.

At that moment, the two men sat in the cramped quarters reserved for junior-grade bachelor officers. Located in a large log-and-mud building beside the parade field, the room was nine feet wide and 14 feet long, with a scant seven feet between the ceiling and floor. Tom's saber and forage cap hung on wooden pegs beside the door. There was a narrow iron bedstead with a shuck mattress, its legs set in four bowls of kerosene to keep the bedbugs off. Besides the bunk and the table, there were two split-bottom chairs, a strap-and-iron trunk, and a washstand with a metal bowl. Corner shelves of crossed sticks held a few leather-bound books. Fly specks clouded the only window.

"I read about the train in the daily reports," Tom said. "Evidently Col. Peatross did make it a

Orphan Train

priority, and he sent Carlson with a platoon. But the fort is short of pony soldiers right now. My men have all been in the field for over a month. They won't be assigned to combat right away unless it's a full-bore emergency.

"It's clear what's happening. Carlson named Touch the Sky as the renegade leading the attack on the kids. That means Touch the Sky must already be trying to help those kids. Now, with this so-called attack on Bighorn Falls, Carlson has been called back. Peatross has advised the territorial militia they might have to step in to help the kids. I'll tell you right now, if that bunch of drunken sots mounts a rescue, all those kids will wind up dead."

"What can we do?" Corey asked. "You're confined to post. With Carlson deliberately sandbagging, Big Tree and the rest of them murderers are enjoying a Green River rendezvous. Touch the Sky must be up against it something fierce."

"You ever known him to be anything but?" Tom Riley spoke absently, his mind having just seized on an idea. "Say, what is it we've got to do here?"

"Damned if I know, Tom. That's why I'm asking you."

"Use the brain God gave you, boy! One thing we've got to do is to get Peatross to put me, not Carlson, in charge of this rescue. These are orphans. He figures nobody cares that much; so he won't send me right away—not with the town in danger. One death of a citizen in his jurisdiction could ruin his retirement pay."

"I catch your drift," Corey said. "We got to make it so somebody does care about them kids. That way, pressure will be on your C.O. to save 'em."

"Right as rain."

"But how?" Corey said. "You can't even leave the post."

"No need to. We got a Flying Telegraph."

Tom meant the Flying Telegraph Train, two mobile wagons loaded with equipment for a portable telegraph system. Its magnetoelectric field had a limited range, but could reach several civilian telegraph offices around Fort Bates.

"I know the telegraphy officer," Tom said, warming to his own idea. "Since I've got plenty of his markers from poker games, I'll strike a deal with him. We'll wire to Register Cliffs."

"To who? They already passed the problem along to the fort."

"Sure. But I'll bet a sawbuck nobody told Nat Trilby about this great human-interest story on the perilous frontier."

Corey's worried face burst into an ear-to-ear grin. "I plumb forgot about ol' Trilby. He's one of the most popular newspapermen in the West!"

"That he is," Tom said, scraping his chair back and grabbing his hat off its peg. "They say he can jerk tears out of a prickly pear. Man's got a nose for a story like a hound for a blood trail. Let's go send him a telegram."

Chapter Nine

Pale moonlight greeted Touch the Sky as he edged slowly out from the passenger coach onto the narrow platform over the coupling that linked them to the coach behind. Touch the Sky was reasonably sure no one lay in waiting close to the train. Nonetheless, he moved quickly to cover the gap to the next car, knowing the renegades could get off a shot if they spotted him.

Again he glanced up toward that ridge, wondering if his band could indeed see at that angle. He removed the flint and steel from his possibles bag and struck a slicing downward blow with the steel against the flint. A brief shower of sparks leapt out. Moments later, sparks answered from the ridge. Touch the Sky took some comfort in that reassuring sight. But as he reached forward

Judd Cole

to open the door of this last passenger car, his back broke out in a cold sweat.

There was a dead man inside, of course. That crew member had been killed defending the train. Touch the Sky had already seen him. And a man didn't have to be an Indian to be nervous about entering a place where death was. But the present problem was different. His shaman eye was watching out for him.

For a long moment Touch the Sky stood out of sight of his enemies, but he didn't enter the coach. He let the fingers of his right hand rest on the beautiful necklace of grizzly claws that Honey Eater had given him as a marriage gift. Arrow Keeper had appeared to her in a dream and instructed her to give the necklace to Touch the Sky. The medicine in the claws was strong, and the warrior drew strength from the claws.

Thus fortified, he slipped inside the car. The Cheyenne stood there, letting his senses read the area. He patiently let his eyes adjust to the dimmer lighting. His ears listened for the slightest sound of movement. His nose sampled the air; a tiny prickle of fear swept along his spine because he sniffed the lingering odor of rancid bear grease, which Sis-ki-dee liked to wear in his hair.

So the renegade had infiltrated the train! Touch the Sky forced himself to remain calm. The smell, he reasoned, would linger whether or not Sis-ki-dee was still on the coach. But Sis-ki-

Orphan Train

dee could be in the caboose. Or he could be in the front coach.

No, Touch the Sky insisted to himself. To make it to the front coach, where the kids were, Sis-ki-dee would either have to go past Touch the Sky or risk fire from the ridge by boarding from outside.

No. There were three possibilities: Sis-ki-dee was no longer on the train, he was in the caboose, or he was in that car with Touch the Sky. The first possibility seemed remote. Why would he bother sneaking on board only to leave again? So either he was in the caboose or within striking range of Touch the Sky.

A quick glance showed the warrior the form of the dead paleface slumped over the back of a seat about halfway down the car. Touch the Sky made the cutoff sign and quickly glanced away since evil spirits could enter the body through a man's eyes.

Touch the Sky calmed his breathing and slid his obsidian knife from its sheath. Then he moved slowly forward, stalking the most fearsome killer in the entire Red Nation.

Hush had not been too scared when Touch the Sky first left to search the train. But as time passed and he heard nothing, he began to get nervous.

The boy moved slowly, vigilantly up and down the aisle, stepping carefully over and around the sleeping children. The Colt was gripped tight in his right fist. He was determined to remember the Cheyenne's instructions to just point and shoot, not to bother aiming. He also had to hoard his shots: one bullet, one enemy.

But what good would the puny little gun be against that band of well-armed savages? Hush remembered reading about something called the unwritten order of the West: Men were supposed to kill women rather than let them be captured by Indians. Was that true for children, too?

Suddenly, something struck the side of the coach, and Hush leapt inches off the floor in fright. The sound hadn't been loud or big. Hush wondered if he'd heard a moccasined foot hitting the coach.

"Tommy?"

"What?"

"You awake?"

"No, I'm talking in my sleep!"

"Didja make that noise?" Hush said.

"I thought it was you."

"Maybe it's just Touch the Sky moving around," Hush said, not sounding too convinced.

When Hush heard the noise again, he whispered, "Spider? That isn't you playing the larks on us with Mr. Wiggle-Wobble, is it?"

Spider's frightened voice answered out of the grainy half-light of the coach. "Mr. Wiggle-Wobble is asleep."

"All right," Hush said, hearing the sound twice

Orphan Train

more, "whoever is doing that had best bring it to a screeching halt before I kick some butt."

Then Hush heard an eerie, high-pitched, mocking laughter. The boy could not tell if it came from outside the car or inside. Fear slammed into him, and his hand gripping his Colt broke out in sweat.

"Who is that?" Hush said.

Again the low, mocking laughter turned Hush's blood as cold as ice.

Methodically, relentlessly, Touch the Sky launched a thorough search of the last coach before the caboose. He left no space, no nook unexamined, but he found nothing. His heart hammering against his ribs, he gripped his knife hard and flung open the door leading to the last coupling platform—the one leading to the caboose.

A figure leapt wildly at Touch the Sky, and he thrust his knife hand toward it, falling back from the attack. The warrior fell hard to the metal platform, jarring his head and back. The figure landed atop him. But immediately the frightened brave's fear transformed itself to anger. Sis-ki-dee had humiliated him once again. The attacker was a buckskin suit stuffed with bunchgrass. It had been propped up with a stick and rigged to fall when the door was opened.

His lips set in a grim, determined slit, Touch the Sky threw the grass enemy aside and waited

Judd Cole

for his breathing to settle down. Then he eased into the caboose, knowing there was nothing else to do. He didn't really expect to find Sis-ki-dee there despite the lingering smell of bear grease. His shaman sense told him the contrary warrior would not do something so predictable as lie in wait for him.

No, Sis-ki-dee would go on the offensive. And Sis-ki-dee would not simply kill without first striking terror into his victims. That grass-stuffed suit was only an example of his handiwork.

Nonetheless, the caboose had to be searched for food and weapons, if nothing else. The car was smaller than the rest. The ghostly moonlight revealed an old Franklin stove and several bunks projecting from the walls. Touch the Sky spotted an old wooden equipment chest near the middle of the car. He was about to lift the lid when he heard a buzzing rattle from inside. More of Sis-ki-dee's work.

Touch the Sky ignored the chest and quickly searched the rest of the coach. Anything of use had already been taken by the renegades. Frustrated, Touch the Sky backed out of the coach again. His eyes fell on the metal rungs leading to the top of the car. Moving slowly, he climbed up and eased his head over the top of the next car.

He could see all the way down to the front of the occupied coach. Sis-ki-dee had not passed him, and he could not have risked that open moonlight to sneak up alongside the train. No

Orphan Train

need to worry, Touch the Sky assured himself. That front coach must be safe.

Suddenly, Touch the Sky's face drained cold as he realized his stupid mistake. There was indeed one more way Sis-ki-dee could have approached that car, one that would leave him hidden from Touch the Sky's band on that ridge.

Quickly the warrior climbed back down the ladder and lowered himself to the ground. He crouched, peering under the car along the gravel bed of the tracks. But it was as dark as midnight down there. Yet how had he forgotten that possibility? Touch the Sky wondered. Ironically, he himself had crawled under train cars to defeat Sis-ki-dee and his men in the Sans Arcs.

Touch the Sky recoiled at the thought of crawling into that dark tunnel under the train. Yet his shaman sense insisted Sis-ki-dee was near. Hush had not sent a signal, nor had any of the children cried for help. So at that point it was reasonably safe to assume Sis-ki-dee had not yet entered the car. Best to rout him out and to take the bull by the horns.

Feeling as if he were lowering himself into a lion's den, Touch the Sky eased under the coupling and flattened himself. He clamped his knife in his teeth, then began the slow, agonizing crawl forward into the lethal darkness.

At the sound of the mocking laughter, Hush had been on the verge of firing his Colt out the window to summon Touch the Sky. But then he remembered what the Cheyenne had told him: He and the other boys would have to stand in for men. And men didn't cry for help every time they were scared. He had to be a leader! Those kids depended on him. And Touch the Sky was counting on him to get the job done.

The first thing was to get the kids quiet. That eerie laugh had woken some of the little ones up, and they were whimpering and crying.

"Spider," he said, "doesn't Mr. Wiggle-Wobble feel like singing something?"

Soon the soft but comforting strains of "Listen to the Mockingbird" calmed the children. But Hush wasn't comforted. He had heard more thumps and the stinging rattle of pebbles being thrown against the car.

"Okay," he said to the kids as he prowled the coach, "let's play a game. Everybody take somebody else's hand. That's it. Everybody holds on to somebody. Sarah, you grab onto Charlie's hand. That's it. Now, even though it's dark, we're all together."

With the kids thus as safe as he could get them, Hush made the tough decision to take a quick peek through the door at the back of the coach. For one thing, Touch the Sky had been gone a long time. Was he hurt?

Hush gripped the metal latch and turned it, easing the door open. The ugliest and scariest face he had ever seen was waiting for him in the

Orphan Train

moonlight. Before fear bucked his entire body, Hush took in the ugly scars, and the short and raggedly cropped hair, the big brass rings dangling from the nose and ears.

"Death to the white man!" the monster hissed, raising a cruel-looking knife with blood and gore still dripping from its blade!

Hush let loose a banshee howl of pure fright. The monster leapt into the next coach even as Hush pointed the Colt and snapped off a round.

Touch the Sky had been somewhat comforted, at first, when he heard the dim strains of the children singing out ahead of him.

Good boy, Hush, he told himself. Keep their minds occupied.

Only halfway through his hard crawl, Touch the Sky's elbows and knees bled profusely. But so far there was no sign of Sis-ki-dee. Yet where else could the renegade be? He wasn't in either of the cars Touch the Sky had checked, nor was he on the train. That left only the bottom. But with Sis-ki-dee, normal logic didn't apply.

Touch the Sky continued his grim journey, frustrated because he felt he was wasting his time, yet knowing it had to be done. Then, above the singing came new sounds: a boy's piercing scream of abject fear, fast footsteps pounding through the coach above him, and the sudden explosion of a gun! Sis-ki-dee had struck!

Touch the Sky's heart crawled into his throat.

Judd Cole

Flinging all caution to the wind, the warrior rolled out from under the coach, leapt to his feet, and sprinted toward the occupied car. Immediately the renegades opened fire on him. Crouching to minimize the target, Touch the Sky sang his death song even as he hurtled toward the coach.

Chapter Ten

"I would not swear to it at council," Little Horse said, his voice tight with worry, "but I think our shaman has once again eluded death."

He, Tangle Hair, and Two Twists had watched, helpless to aid their leader as he risked the flurry of bullets to gain the coach.

"I saw him climb into the little lodge on wheels," Two Twists said. "But, buck, they rained bullets on him! Maiyun grant he was not hit because he will need his wits about him to survive."

"How many more times," Little Horse said bitterly, "can he knock the Grim Warrior from his pony? Touch the Sky has never known a full sleep's peace in his life! When he lived among the whites, they scorned him and called him a preying Indian. And every moment among the red

Judd Cole

men, he is reminded that he once wore white man's shoes. Now, so soon after this good news about his child, his life is at risk."

"And we cannot draw a bead on our enemy to help him!" Tangle Hair said. "I see how it is now. Big Tree's ride earlier was not mere sport meant to remind us Cheyennes which tribe truly invented mounted warfare. That bold charge covered for the Red Peril. He is on that train!"

"Yes," Little Horse said. "I fear Sis-ki-dee may have added to his gruesome legacy of terror by killing another child. And if the Red Peril is truly aboard that iron horse, more will die. What can we do, brothers? I am not one to sit in my tipi when my comrades ride the war path!"

"Nor I," said Tangle Hair, the most levelheaded of the trio. "But, brothers, we dare not send a rider back to camp. It is foolish enough for three of us to think we can stop the charge, if the renegades put the trance glaze over their eyes and rush. Two will surely be defeated."

"Straight words, buck," Little Horse said. "We could persuade some of Spotted Tail's Bow Strings to ride here. But think of that many-muzzled rifle firing into our comrades and leaving scores of widows back in our camp."

"As you say. But look how little ammunition we have, how little food. And below, they may have none."

Little Horse nodded. "You are right. We will remain here and take our chances with the brave

Bear Caller. We cannot give up the high ground. It is all we have. I know I speak for all of us when I say that I have sworn my loyalty and my very life to him and his struggle. When Seth Carlson's bullet found my lights up in the Bear Paws, Touch the Sky put his own breath in my dead nostrils and nursed back the spark of life in me."

"And think," Two Twists said, pride evident in his voice if not his moonlit face since warriors kept their feelings private. "When Mountain Fever laid our tribe low, Touch the Sky rode into the Valley of Sorrow itself to obtain white man's medicine. Near death himself from his journey, he gave strength to the white man's magic by setting up a pole and hanging from it. Those hooks came a gnat's width from killing him. But he cried out to Maiyun, and the Day Maker took pity on our people."

"Speak the truth and shame the Wendigo," Little Horse said. "Now we must help our brother and those children. Bucks, I tell you I despise many in the white race. But I hold their children innocent and as worthy of life as our own. If our comrade dies and those little ones with him, let their ghosts never say that we three rode away to live!"

All three crossed their lances in the moonlight, and Little Horse said, "Enough of vows. Now comes the hard slogging. Gather what pemmican you have. Just before Sister Sun claims the sky, I will ride down fast and throw it into the little lodge. Until then, let us have done with speech and keep our thoughts nothing but bloody. I tell you—and this place hears me—the fight is coming."

"That face you saw," Touch the Sky said, "belonged to Sis-ki-dee, a Blackfoot renegade from the north country."

"Damn but he was ugly," Hush said, shivering at the memory. "And mean? That was the face of a man who steals dead flies from blind spiders."

"He's past that," Touch the Sky said. "He's a low-down, thieving, murdering renegade. If you hadn't stayed cool enough to shoot at him, he probably would have killed you."

Even in the moonlight, Touch the Sky saw Hush pale at the thought. They were hunkered together toward the middle of the coach. The dawn star was low in the east, and there was perhaps another hour before daybreak.

"Where is he now?" Hush said nervously. "Still on the train?"

Touch the Sky nodded grimly. "He is a master at concealment and patient as a snake when it comes to waiting for the kill. As you have already discovered, he is also a master at creating terror in his victims."

"Touch the Sky, how much longer can this go on? Where is the army or the constables?"

"This isn't New York City, Hush. There's a marshal in Laramie, but he doesn't trouble with In-

Orphan Train

dians unless there's a complaint against them from whites. Around here, it's mostly the army that serves as law. And the army is like a chain. It's only as good as its weakest link. The army hereabouts has a very weak link named Seth Carlson."

"Well, pretty soon will start our second day here. Won't another train come by?"

"Sure, but not for a few days. There's a spur line south of the Platte that gets more traffic."

A child whimpered in his sleep and Touch the Sky grimaced. If his belly was gnawing at him from hunger, what must theirs be doing? Luckily Esther Buchanan had left behind a canvas water bag. Through strict rationing, Touch the Sky had been able to give each child a few mouthfuls to tide them over. But they were completely out of food except for a sack of stale corn dodgers.

Hush took off his battered bowler hat and swiped the perspiration off his forehead. "They got our heads in the wringer, ain't they?"

Touch the Sky couldn't help smiling at the youth. Life on the streets had taught him how to sound so old and tough, but it hadn't destroyed his courage or his protective instincts. Touch the Sky had noticed how carefully Hush kept track of every child, how vigilantly he studied the landscape outside those windows, watching for the attack. The boy was scared spitless, but he would die like a man protecting his younger charges.

"It looks grim," Touch the Sky said. "We've got

Judd Cole

the worst killer in the Indian Nation on board this train with us. And there might be thirty Indian hard cases waiting to rush us. But we Cheyennes have a saying: The fight isn't over until the last Cheyenne is dead.

"We send out warriors to fight our battles, Hush. But when our camp is attacked, any man, woman, or child capable of holding a stick or throwing a rock becomes a warrior. I have seen Cheyenne women throw and scalp mounted warriors, and I have watched children swarm on a soldier like enraged bees."

"Yeah, but them's Indians."

"The same heart beats in every human breast, Hush. What red kids can do, white kids can do."

"I suppose but—"

A sudden roll of hoofbeats sent Touch the Sky and Hush leaping to the windows. But it wasn't their enemy attacking. In the clear moonlight, Touch the Sky saw Little Horse's tough piebald hurtling down the slope from the ridge. Renegade rifles began cracking, and arrows tipped with the white man's deadly sheet iron turned the air dangerous all around Little Horse. The brave slid forward into the defensive riding position; only his head was visible down beneath the pony's neck.

"What's he doing?" Hush said. "They'll kill him!"

"So what?" Touch the Sky said, the Indian's proud defiance clear in his voice as he watched this brave friend. "That one does not fear death.

He will sit behind no man at council in the Land of Ghosts!"

Outwitting death at every step, Little Horse flew straight at the train. At the last possible moment, he reined his pony hard. As the sturdy little brave flashed past the windows on his return ride, he hurled a buckskin parfleche through a window. It sailed past Hush's nose by inches and smacked into the wall behind him.

"Pemmican," Touch the Sky said, opening the parfleche. "Not much, but it is nourishing. This will have to do."

"Pemmi-what?" Hush said, staring dubiously at the dark strips that resembled jerked beef.

"Pemmican is buffalo meat that's been dried in the sun and cut thin. Our women pound it with a maul and mix it with fat, marrow, and dried cherry paste. Pemmican gets us through the winters."

"What's it taste like?"

"Damn good if you're hungry enough. You'll find out when I give all of you your share for breakfast. For now, though, get some rest."

Too tired to object, Hush curled up right there on the floor, pulling his pea jacket over him against the fall chill. "Touch the Sky?"

"Hm?"

"Do you think Sis-ki-dee was planning to come into this car when I bumped into him?"

"Maybe, but never mind now. You scared him off. Just rest."

Touch the Sky, too, let himself drift in and out

of a light doze, knowing Sis-ki-dee would not strike again that night. Touch the Sky had just thrown back his head, letting his weary eyes shut, as the first saffron beams of new sun broke over the Black Hills to the east. But Sarah Pettigrew's scream of abject horror brought him flying wildly to his feet, knife in hand. Hush, too, jumped up, Colt at the ready.

Sarah's scream woke all the rest of the children. When Touch the Sky joined them in looking where she pointed, he felt his blood run cold. Dangling from the emergency-brake cord at the front of the coach was the severed human head of a white man!

"Have ears for my words," Wolf Who Hunts Smiling said.

Dawn had only recently painted the eastern sky in salmon-pink strokes. Wolf Who Hunts Smiling and Big Tree stood in the shelter of a boulder, looking out at the stranded train.

"With Sis-ki-dee on that train," Wolf Who Hunts Smiling said, "the victory is ours if we are only men enough to be patient a bit longer. Those children and Woman Face cannot continue to hold out. And once Sis-ki-dee guts Woman Face, the children will be on their own. Those three on the ridge will be nothing without their leader."

"Sis-ki-dee is capable," Big Tree said. "But he is indeed contrary. I know that one. He will pass up the opportunity to kill quickly in favor of terrorizing his victims. He is having great sport, but what of our ransom money?"

"We can wait," Wolf Who Hunts Smiling said. "Just a bit longer. No iron horse is due through here for two more sleeps. Seth Carlson has sent word that his plan went well. His big eagle chief has ordered him to remain near Bighorn Falls. Your men did a good job of striking the fear of wild Indians into the white-livered cowards who live there."

"We must hurry," Big Tree said. "The whites called the territorial militia will soon ride here from Laramie if no one else saves these children."

"Eventually, yes. You speak straight. But word is slow to get around. And truly, Quohada, so what if they do come? So what if we do not get our money? If we see that hair faces are about to rescue these whelps, we will simply kill all of them and flee."

Big Tree flashed his big, strong teeth in a grin. "I have ears for this! We kill them, and the massacre of white children will be laid at the tipi entrance of the Bear Caller."

"Now your thoughts drift with mine. The portents are finally going our way. His squaw is keeping his child a secret, but we have been warned the seed is inside her and growing. We will not only kill Touch the Sky. We will also destroy his spawn."

Big Tree nodded, his weather-seamed face inscrutable in the early light. "By this time tomorrow, it should all be over."

Chapter Eleven

Shortly after Horace Greeley, editor of the *New York Herald*, sent Nat Trilby out beyond the hundredth meridian as a Western stringer, Trilby became the most popular frontier journalist in America. Trilby's exciting accounts of life on the wild frontier gave most Americans east of the Mississippi their notion of what life was like out there in Zebulon Pike's Great American Desert. Trilby was a wily man who knew his audience well. The citizens of the young nation were a practical lot who knew you couldn't eat ideas; yet they were also ridiculously sentimental and loved a good melodrama. And the story of the stranded orphans—Trilby told himself as he edited his final version of the article—made for terrific melodrama.

Orphan Train

It was just after sunup, and Trilby had worked most of the night on the story, ever since Tom Riley's telegram had been delivered to his dingy little walk-up in the Commerce Hotel. Trilby had only a few basic facts—the who, the what, the when, the where, and most importantly, the why—but that was enough basis to weave a first-rate tearjerker.

He looked tired and drawn in the light from a lard-oil lamp. But the work had been worth the extra effort, he thought as he ran his eye down the neatly handwritten pages of foolscap. What a story! After Greeley read the article, he would double Trilby's remittance payments.

The title itself was brilliant: *What About Bub And Sis?* The term bub and sis, brother and sister, was currently the fashionable way back east of referring to children one did not know.

" 'Are these unfortunate waifs,' " Trilby said, reading his story out loud, since he was always one to appreciate his own prose, " 'less human, less Christian, because they have been abandoned? No! In truth, their struggle against lawless, murdering savages symbolizes the larger American struggle. These orphans epitomize the Yankee pluck and courage that wrought this young nation out of the raw materials of the New World.' "

Trilby laid the sheets down. "Oh, dear," he said, "they're going to raise Cain back in the States!"

The weary journalist pulled his watch out of his fob pocket and slid back the cover with his thumb. Not yet 7 a.m. If he hurried, he could deliver the article to the office of the *Register Gazette* in time for that day's edition. Then he would file the story by telegraphic dispatch. Just a few years earlier, several major newspapers, his included, had formed the Associated Press for sharing telegraphic dispatches. Soon the story would be read and repeated all across the republic.

Trilby picked up his quill, dipped it, and quickly added the numeral 30 to the bottom of his last page, marking the end of the article for the editor and typesetter. Then he hurried down into the streets of Register Cliffs, brimming with ambition to stir up a sensation and ensure his fame.

"Damn it, Carlson. If you don't stop being so mealymouthed, I'm assigning you to four-holer detail!" Col. Peatross said.

"But, sir, you—"

"Stow it, Captain! And you, Riley! Wipe that smile off your face! You're at attention."

"Yes, sir!"

Riley did as ordered. The situation was not humorous. But he couldn't hold back his grin when he realized his strategy had worked. There lay Nat Trilby's story, prominently boxed on page one of the *Gazette*, on top the C.O.'s desk. And

Orphan Train

shitheel Carlson was on the carpet again.

"One more time," Col. Peatross said. "Carlson, why have you taken no action to help those children?"

"Sir, the Colonel himself called my unit back from that mission to protect the citizens of Bighorn Falls from further Indian attacks. That's what we've been doing."

"No, it's not. I'll tell you what your men have been doing in Bighorn Falls. They've been drinking, whoring, and gambling, and you've been leading the pack. Was there ever a subsequent attack after that first strike?"

"No, sir. But—"

"Keep your buts to yourself, mister. Did you send out patrols to trail these marauders?"

"No, sir. I assumed it was best to protect the town, not play hero."

"Damn noble of you," Tom said sarcastically, unable to restrain himself in the face of such cowardly hypocrisy.

Carlson sent him a withering glance. "If you're feeling froggy, Riley, you just jump!"

"Stow it!" Angry blood flushed Peatross's face. He came to his feet. "Both of you, stow it and listen to me. I've already been visited by the mayor of Register Cliffs. He's outraged. That man is as tough as saddle leather, yet this story left tears in his eyes! Those kids must be rescued. Is that clear?"

"Yes, sir," Carlson said before Riley could

speak. "My men are ready and up to unit strength while Capt. Riley's are not. I suggest sending his platoon into town to take over the guard duty while my platoon takes care of this business with the train."

"Bad idea, sir," Riley cut in. "There's no danger in town, and I have no drunkards in my unit! Send us, and this time the objective will be accomplished in short order."

"Drunkards?" Carlson said. "Nothing worse than a platoon commander who's an Indian lover!"

"Shut up, both of you," Peatross said. "Carlson is right. His unit is up to manual strength. But if you mess this thing up one more time, Captain, I'm not just sending Riley to get it done. I'm making sure your career in this man's army is over. Is that clear?"

"Yes, sir!"

"Colonel," Tom said, "don't send Carlson. Let me handle this."

"Are those railroad tracks I see on your shoulders or silver eagles?" Peatross said. "When you have a star up there, son, you can give the orders around here. Now you've got your orders. Go carry them out. Dismissed!"

It had taken Touch the Sky quite some time to calm the children again after the grisly discovery of a human head dangling at the front of the coach. It was actually Hush who first recognized

Orphan Train

that the head had belonged to the dead man back in the coach behind them. Gritting his teeth and averting his eyes, Touch the Sky had detached the horrible thing and flung it out the windows.

But that terrifying discovery was far more than simply disgusting. Its real import, Touch the Sky realized, was to prove that Sis-ki-dee could move like a shadow and infiltrate their position at will.

Outside, the sun tracked higher. When the children were calmed, Touch the Sky carefully divided the pemmican Little Horse had thrown to them. Some were reluctant to bite into the oddly textured food. But once Hush pronounced the pemmican a huckleberry above your average persimmon, the rest tied in with gusto.

With the children quieted, Touch the Sky turned to the most serious problem at hand: Sis-ki-dee. Touch the Sky could not be sure the renegade was still on the train. But there was a good chance he was. If so, the patient stalker might rest and wait to strike again that night. Or if time was against him, he might make a bold move by daylight. Clearly, however, cutting off dead men's heads or even hurting the children was not the priority. Killing Touch the Sky was.

It was not the Cheyenne way to hide and play the hunted once marked out for death; rather, a Cheyenne went on the offensive and turned the fight back around on the attacker. Touch the Sky had no desire to simply wait for death to come to him. It would be better to die routing the Grim

Warrior from his black pony.

"I have to search the train again," Touch the Sky said.

Hush's face paled. "Last time you done that, that Sis-ki-shit paid us a visit."

"He had darkness to help him slip past me. He won't this time. In broad daylight like this, my brothers on that ridge can spot any movement under or on top of the train. He'll have to pass me or them."

Hush nodded, though he didn't seemed completely convinced, and Touch the Sky said, "After you fired your piece, did you charge the empty cylinder?"

Hush nodded. "I capped it, too."

"Good man. You scared him off once. You can do it again. If I hear that pistol go off, I'll be back here quicker than scat. That's a promise."

Touch the Sky took one last look around. Some of the children had gone back to sleep; others lay huddled, quietly talking.

"Careful," Touch the Sky said to six-year-old Charlie Brace. "Keep your head below those windows."

Touch the Sky was reluctant to leave the children again. But he was even more reluctant to let Sis-ki-dee play the game on his own terms. So once again he launched his methodical search.

Knife gripped in his fist, every sense alert, the tall Cheyenne slipped into the car behind theirs. His repugnance to enter that car where death

Orphan Train

dwelt was heightened by the knowledge that the corpse's head had been severed. Yet he forced himself to a thorough search before finally moving on to the caboose.

As if waiting for the moment when Touch the Sky was farthest from the children, the renegades launched an attack in force. War cries and thundering hooves filled the air; the screaming Requa battery hurled volley after volley into the train; bullets and arrows peppered it. Touch the Sky heard the kids screaming even as he threw caution to the wind and jumped outside of the caboose, racing on foot for the lead car.

For a few moments he saw all of the attack as clearly as if it were a painted tableau. The renegades raced out from the headland behind the train, and his little band charged down from the ridge in front. A frightened but determined Hush Cochran boldly took up a position at a window despite the lead and arrows screaming around his ears.

The renegades pounded closer behind the fleeing Touch the Sky, narrowing the gap even as he desperately tried to reach that front coach. He glanced over his shoulder just in time to see a wildly racing Comanche raise his deadly stone skull cracker.

Still on the run, Touch the Sky raised and threw his knife in one smooth overhand movement. It sliced into the screaming Comanche's belly just beneath his bone breastplate, not killing him but taking the fight out of him. The Comanche slumped in the saddle.

Touch the Sky had almost gained the door of the coach. But a second renegade bore down on him. Tangle Hair, charging from the opposite direction, let loose his war lance. It skewered the renegade and lifted him neatly from his horse.

As Touch the Sky leapt for the platform between the coaches, he saw yet another renegade jump up at the opposite end, reaching for the door. Hush's Colt roared, the savage's face disappeared in a smear of scarlet, and the dead Kiowa folded to the tracks.

"C'mon, you savages!" the youth bellowed. "There's more where that come from!"

Then Little Horse's revolving four-barrel shotgun started blasting as the reckless brave rode into the teeth of the assault. With three more renegades killed, his assault was enough to break the attack.

"We did it!" Hush shouted to the Cheyenne. "Look! They're pulling foot!"

"You fought like five men," Touch the Sky said. "You even defied your enemy while you were doing it. Wouldn't take me long to turn you into a good Cheyenne warrior."

Hush puffed himself up with pride at these words. However, their elation was short-lived. Touch the Sky had forgotten, in all this excitement, about the missing Sis-ki-dee. But Sis-ki-

Orphan Train

dee had not forgotten about Touch the Sky and the orphans. Under the diversion of the attack, he had visited once again.

"Do the roll call, Hush," Touch the Sky said. "Make sure all the kids are here and okay."

Hush, who knew all the kids, called their names off one by one. Each answered in turn until Hush checked for Charlie Brace. When no response came from little Charlie, someone said, "He's asleep. I'll wake him up."

"No!" Touch the Sky shouted, a sudden and queasy premonition icing his blood. "Let me do it."

Charlie still lay where Touch the Sky had last seen him, huddled under a seat in the middle of the car. The warrior knelt and shook the boy, but he got no response. Gently, his heart fear-hammering, Touch the Sky rolled the silent youth over and saw the deep, ragged gash where Sis-ki-dee had slashed Charlie's throat.

Chapter Twelve

"Aunt," a worried Honey Eater said, "when Sister Sun goes to her rest, it will be two sleeps since Touch the Sky and his band rode out. Why have we heard nothing?"

"Why?" Sharp Nosed Woman let her beadwork fall into her lap. The two women sat before the entrance flap of Sharp Nosed Woman's tipi. "Child, do you know what Old Woman Dress of the Coyote Clan does when her children ask why?"

Honey Eater shook her head. A moment later her eyes widened in indignant surprise when her aunt reached across and slapped her cheek! Honey Eater started to protest. Then, at the sly smile on her aunt's face, she gave in to a smile herself. "I understand. Perhaps it is not wise for a Cheyenne to ask why."

"Now you talk like your mother," Sharp Nosed Woman said, making the cutoff sign by moving one hand diagonally in front of her body. "The last woman with sense in this tribe passed over when Pawnees killed her."

"I cannot pretend that I do not love my husband," Honey Eater said, "or that I do not worry about him."

"Worry about him? Honey Eater, have you ever done anything else? Now here you are with—" Sharp Nosed Woman caught herself and glanced around. Then she lowered her voice. "Now here you are with child and still worrying. Do you not remember the mothering way taught you in the domestic lodge? The thoughts of the mother spark those of the child. A mother who lusts during gestation spawns a lustful child. Yours will worry to death! Niece, you are not living for your tall warrior alone now, but also for your child."

Sharp Nosed Woman's words were true enough, and they only made Honey Eater's pretty face wrinkle more as her frown deepened. Truly, she wanted nothing more than to be a wife worthy of her brave and the best possible mother for her child. But as Touch the Sky's disappearance only proved once again, there were no peaceful thoughts possible for her. She would do her best, but only a stone heart could not but worry.

"Do not look up," Sharp Nosed Woman said in a low voice, "but the bone blower is watching you again. Honey Eater, it is not your fault that, in a tribe known for its beauties, you were born to lead the procession. This Medicine Flute has fire in his loins for you. I fear the issue of his lust. And Maiyun help him if Touch the Sky ever sees him looking at you as he is right now."

"When my husband is in camp," Honey Eater said, "no one shows disrespect to me, least of all this pretend shaman who mocks the Holy Ones by his very being. He is a coward, a white liver who would hold a child in front of him to stop a bullet. I only wish his master, Wolf Who Hunts Smiling, were just such a coward. But he is covered with hard bark and has no soft place left in him."

"I once felt sorry for that wily Wolf," Sharp Nosed Woman said. "When he was still an unblooded youth, he watched as bluecoat canister shot turned his father into raw meat before his very eyes. His hatred for the whites thus knows no bounds. As for your husband, I have never known a better Cheyenne. But he has one unpardonable sin against him, in the eyes of our Wolf Who Hunts Smiling. He was raised by whites."

"He, too, has been gone much," Honey Eater said. She was so deeply mired in apprehension that she even forgot that Medicine Flute was again staring at her. "Whatever treachery has kept Touch the Sky and the rest from camp, Wolf Who Hunts Smiling is its cause."

The nature of Wolf Who Hunts Smiling's treachery soon became clear to Honey Eater. Later that morning, the excited camp crier raced his pony up and down the village paths, announcing that the trading party recently sent to the post at Red Shale was returning. That news brought the entire camp into the central clearing and created a holiday mood. However, Honey Eater soon realized their return actually foretold great trouble. As the party rode into camp, led by River of Winds, she noticed their travois. They were indeed piled high, but not with bolts of cloth, kegs of powder, or packets of flour and sugar and coffee. Instead, they were still loaded with the beaver plews and beadwork-embroidered clothing the tribe had sent to trade.

Honey Eater watched Chief Gray Thunder walked forth from the crowd and address River of Winds. "The whole world knows that beaver fur is not so valuable now that the foolish hair faces have changed the fashion of their hats. But, River of Winds, no women from where I stand now to the sun's resting place are more highly praised for the art of their beadwork than ours! Those garments there should have brought us enough powder and lead for two hunts. Yet like starving curs they have returned to their tribe. Speak words I can pick up and examine! What means this?"

"Father, how many times have we smoked the common pipe together? These lips that speak to you now touched that pipe. You will hear nothing but truth from me."

River of Winds paused, and Honey Eater felt a shiver of apprehension tickle her spine when his eyes met hers and then quickly flicked away again.

"Father! Brothers! Have ears! The white traders at Red Shale have declared they will no longer accept any goods from Gray Thunder's tribe!"

River of Winds was forced to pause when an explosion of angry disbelief sounded from the rest. The Bull Whip troopers gathered around Medicine Flute were especially vocal. Gray Thunder folded his arms, the gesture commanding silence.

River of Winds went on. "They still accept goods from other tribes and even from the other bands of the Cheyenne. But none from us."

"Why?" Lone Bear, leader of the Whips, demanded.

"Because they claim renegades from our tribe have attacked an iron horse that was bringing white children to our land. They claim we mean to either steal these children and sell them for ransom or to murder them."

The accusation was so monstrous an injustice that Gray Thunder had no heart to rebuke the people when they cried out in angry protest.

Orphan Train

"Now," River of Winds said, "Indian fever has been whipped to a frenzy. It is not only the traders who mean to punish us. They talk now of assembling the paleface militia to punish us with an attack on our camp!"

Honey Eater was on the verge of losing all strength in her legs because she had learned to recognize when Touch the Sky's enemies were closing another trap around him. Sharp Nosed Woman saw her niece suddenly turn pale. She put a sympathetic arm around her niece and urged her to be strong. She, too, saw which way the wind set.

Ominously, the entire tribe quieted to dead silence when Medicine Flute slowly walked to the middle of the clearing. He held his leg-bone flute in both hands. "Cheyenne people! He who first made the days and then gave them to us has already sent me a warning. Now I only remind all of you to bear in mind which renegades have been missing from our camp."

"Do you mean," Spotted Tail said, "your master, Wolf Who Hunts Smiling? Truly, that one has been gone much lately."

Honey Eater shivered when she saw Medicine Flute's lazy-lidded gaze turn to pure hatred. "Someone in this tribe must be man enough to watch Woman Face and hold him in check. I notice you speak boldly when Wolf Who Hunts Smiling is off protecting his tribe. You have less to say when he is here to answer for himself.

Your wit is as faint as your manhood."

Medicine Flute turned to River of Winds. "Which renegades?" he demanded. "Whom do they accuse of this crime?"

His question hung in the air like a threat. Honey Eater was not the only one who had noticed how Medicine Flute had boldly usurped Gray Thunder's right to ask this question himself.

Again River of Winds looked to his friend Honey Eater, guilt flickering in his eyes. Then she knew his answer. She also knew that River of Winds had been sent on the mission because no brave in the tribe was more respected for his honesty. So when he finally spoke his words, they landed on her like bluecoat buckshot.

"They mention no names," he said. "But the leader is tall for a Cheyenne, broad shouldered, and heavily muscled like an Apache. And he has three followers. They say the leader rides a speckled medicine-hat mustang."

No uproar came since the enormity of the news had struck many dumb with disbelief.

"River of Winds," Spotted Tail said, "these words trouble me greatly. But have the palefaces proof of this charge?"

"I know not if they have. But we rode past that bluff on our way back to camp. People, the train is there, destroyed as the white men claim!"

Then a clamor did break out. When there was

Orphan Train

some quiet, Medicine Flute's reedy voice cried out, "And did you see Touch the Sky?"

Terrified, Honey Eater realized that River of Winds was miserable.

"Not him," River of Winds replied. "But his medicine-hat mustang was there. And so were Little Horse, Two Twists, and Tangle Hair."

"What were they doing?"

"They appeared to be watching the train."

"Did you see these children?" Lone Bear demanded.

"Yes, glimpses of them trapped on the iron horse."

"Did you see any other Indians?"

Again River of Winds looked trapped. "None from where we were. But we did not dwell on the scene long, nor ride down closer for fear of—"

"For fear of what?" Lone Bear said. "For fear of being killed by our loyal tribesmen?"

River of Winds refused to answer the question. But Honey Eater knew his silence was as damaging as an affirmative.

"This is Touch the Sky's plan for our tribe!" Medicine Flute cried out. "See? See it now? Wolf Who Hunts Smiling spoke straight words all along. Only see how cleverly the tall one works to bring the wrath of the entire white nation down on our tribe!"

But Gray Thunder was determined to avoid a dramatic confrontation like the last one, which had almost erupted in tribal war. He spoke out, putting his deep chest behind the words.

"Cheyenne people! It hardly matters if all these things said about Touch the Sky are true. I do not believe them. But never mind. Do you see, all of you, that at this moment, guilty or not, he is not the issue? We must take some action concerning this iron horse. If those children are harmed, we will all go under!"

Shouts of approval rang out, and Honey Eater felt some measure of relief surge into her numb limbs. The charge against Touch the Sky and his band was preposterous, of course. More strong mushroom talk invented by his enemies. But Gray Thunder's action cleverly gave the entire tribe a sense of urgency to pull together. That night, again, war within the tribe had been avoided. But how much longer could the beleaguered Gray Thunder hold off the inevitable?

The men gathered and headed toward the council lodge for an emergency discussion of the new crisis. The women and elders, full of the shocking news, gathered in their clan circles to discuss it. Even safe inside her aunt's tipi, Honey Eater could feel accusing eyes on her, the woman who loved a traitor to her own people.

"Never mind, child," Sharp Nosed Woman said when tears erupted from Honey Eater's eyes. "Never mind. Maiyun has always found some way to fix the hurting places. He may do so again."

There was some comfort in those words, and Honey Eater gratefully found it. But both women shuddered when they heard right outside the closed entrance flap of the lodge the eerie piping of Medicine Flute's instrument.

Then came the cruelly whispered words that turned both women's faces into masks of frozen horror. "Honey Eater, his child will never breathe life!"

Chapter Thirteen

"It's no good," Carlson said. "My big eagle chief has ordered me to save those children. You'll have to move quick. If you don't, I'll have to take action."

Wolf Who Hunts Smiling frowned, anger smoking his furtive and swift-moving eyes. "Can we not simply attack the town again?"

Carlson shook his head. "Tom Riley's men are guarding town, so it wouldn't matter. Besides, even if I didn't have to do something, the citizen's militia is about to move against you, too."

Wolf Who Hunts Smiling looked at Big Tree. "See, Quohada? Once again we can thank Sis-ki-dee's sick brain for costing us our opportunity. He might have killed Woman Face by now. Instead, he is relishing the sheer pleasure of inflicting terror on those children.

"And now, word comes from Lone Bear that my own tribe has learned of this situation. They are about to send out a war party. The good news is that the blame has been placed squarely on White Man Runs Him. The bad news is that the trap is closing in on us from all around."

Big Tree nodded, his deep-set eyes surveying the train out ahead of him. "It was a good plan. It still is, but we must either get those children or clear out of here. Blue blouse, can you hold back your men until tomorrow?"

Carlson glanced up at the late afternoon sky. "Yes, but no later. Peatross is champing at the bit. And if I sandbag too much longer, he'll send Riley's platoon. I assure you, they won't shoot wide."

"I fear no soldiers," Big Tree said with contempt. "It is common knowledge that white men rut on sheep and turn the offspring into soldiers."

Carlson bit back his reply, knowing either of the two renegades would kill him on a whim.

"Fear is not the issue," Wolf Who Hunts Smiling said. "If Riley comes, those children will be saved. And then the white wrath will not be turned against the Cheyennes so that White Man Runs Him will be the scourge of our tribe. That is why, if we cannot seize the children for ransom by the time Sister Sun rises tomorrow, we must at least kill them."

He crossed to his pure black pony and pulled

a canvas nitro pack from his pannier. "Our last one. If Sis-ki-dee fails to kill Woman Face in time, I will ride hard and toss this under their coach. One bullet will set it off."

Touch the Sky was able to keep most of the children from seeing the horrifying sight of the dead Charlie Brace. But never would he forget the shock of turning that little boy over, nor his failure to protect the child.

His lips set in a grim, determined slit, Touch the Sky carried Charlie to the very back of the car and placed him in the last seat. He removed his buckskin shirt to cover the little boy. When he returned, Hush was still at work calming the others.

Hush saw the guilt and self-loathing on the Cheyenne's face. "Aw, Touch the Sky, it wasn't no fault of yours. That Sis-ki-dee is slippery."

The lad's attempt to raise his spirits made Touch the Sky grin briefly. "You're right, little brother. He moves like a shadow. They say he can steal up to the bed of a sleeping couple and steal the wife without waking the husband. But he's not getting in here again."

"If he ain't here now," Hush said, his eyes sweeping the coach.

Touch the Sky's frustration was extreme. So far he had been able to do little more than watch events unfold. True, it was his presence on the train, as well as the support of his plucky band on that ridge, that had so far held off the renegades. But Touch the Sky was not one for holing up and waiting for events to happen. White men liked to fight from fixed positions; Indians liked to skirmish on the move. The train car was a death trap, pure and simple.

"Damn, I'd like to wrap my teeth around some grub," Hush said. "That pemmican was all right, but there wasn't enough."

A few of the younger children, having quieted from the shock of Charlie's death, whimpered from the hunger gnawing at their bellies. Touch the Sky knew the situation was becoming increasingly desperate. Ammo for Hush's Colt, and for Touch the Sky's friends on the ridge, was low, the last of their water was dwindling, and worst of all, Sis-ki-dee was still unaccounted for. Even as he was cataloging their troubles, a rifle sounded from outside and another jagged shard of window glass fragmented, making Sarah scream.

"Cover down!" Hush shouted, taking command of the kids immediately.

He himself had several sharp cuts on his face from flying glass. Snipers had continually peppered the car, keeping everyone in a state of nervous apprehension. To make matters worse, the renegades had also taken to launching fire arrows into the wooden coach. Fortunately, the linseed-treated wood was slow to catch fire, and so far no serious blazes had erupted. But if one of those fires did catch hold, Touch the Sky knew the wooden coach would go up great guns.

Abruptly, a loud thump from the car behind them cut into Touch the Sky's thoughts. Touch the Sky and Hush locked glances.

"That's him," Hush said, swallowing a hard lump of fear. "That's how he done last time."

Touch the Sky nodded. "Sure isn't mice."

The noise was deliberate; Touch the Sky knew that. Sis-ki-dee moved as silently as the stars across the heavens. The critical question was not who made the noise, but why.

"Listen, Hush, and listen good. Is your pistol loaded and ready?"

Solemnly, the lad checked his weapon. "Yes, sir."

"Good. I'm counting on you again, Hush. Here's the way it is. That noise marks a trap. Either Sis-ki-dee is luring me into the next car so he can kill me, or he's luring me back there so he can sneak in here and kill somebody else. You understand?"

Hush swallowed audibly. "Yes, sir. I gotta keep a sharp eye out. And if that red savage tries to come in here, I got to blow him to Kingdom Come."

Touch the Sky nodded. "Quiet your mind of all thoughts, Hush. Don't think at all because you don't need to. Animals survive by fully attending to the senses God gave them; so do Indians. Just look, listen, and smell."

Orphan Train

"Smell?" Hush almost laughed despite his fear.

"Yes, little brother, smell. Any man can train his nose to smell horses, water at night, or even Indians and soldiers. Sis-ki-dee likes to wear rancid bear grease in his hair. You will not get many warnings with that one. So stay keen and be ready to react instantly."

"Sure you don't want the gun?"

Touch the Sky shook his head and slid his reserve knife from his sash. "The man who kills Sis-ki-dee will not be so lucky as to shoot him. I fought him once with knives. Our left arms were tied together at the wrists. I should have killed him then, but I did not because he fell unconscious. The Cheyenne Way does not permit the killing of a sleeping or unconscious enemy."

"Man alive," Hush said. "No offense, Touch the Sky, I think you're just dandy. But that was a tarnal stupid mistake you made."

Touch the Sky nodded. "No offense taken because you're right. But the past is a dead thing and should be left alone. This isn't the past. Now let's give over with words and talk with action."

But what kind of action? Touch the Sky wondered as he quickly slipped across the platform onto the next car. How did one take action against a shadow, kill an elusive noise, defend against an enemy who was everywhere felt but nowhere seen?

Touch the Sky followed his own advice and

Judd Cole

cleared his head of intrusive thoughts. The stench in there was beginning to worsen as the dead crewman's body started to decay. Touch the Sky gave up trying to locate Sis-ki-dee's distinctive odor.

He waited some time until his eyes had adjusted to the darker coach. Moving his head ever so slowly, he scoured every inch of the coach with his eyes. Then he dropped to the floor and looked under both rows of seats. He stayed down there some time, breathing silently through his open mouth to cut down extraneous noises while he listened closely.

Two odd noises he couldn't quite identify seemed to come from the back of the coach. Slowly, carefully, silently, Touch the Sky moved down the middle aisle, his right hand gripping his knife. Fear made his heart stomp against his ribs, but he commanded himself to control his breathing and remain calm.

Again came a pair of odd sounds he couldn't quite recognize. That time they seemed to come from behind him. Puzzled, Touch the Sky looked over his shoulder. That was when the original noises sounded again from the front of the coach. Startled, he spun around, only to hear two more strange sounds behind him.

"Sis-ki-dee," he said boldly, "I admit I admire you. I mean to kill you. But this place hears me when I say that I will dangle your hair with pride from my coup stick."

Orphan Train

An insane, whispering laugh seemed to emanate from everywhere at once. Ignoring the noises and determined to quit cowering like a mouse in a hole, Touch the Sky continued his search for the entire length of the car. But he found nothing, and the noises stopped.

Beware, whispered a warning voice inside Touch the Sky's skull, he is sneaking onto the coach with the children!

Fear slammed into the warrior like a body blow. Touch the Sky spun on his heel, raced back toward the platform, flung open the door, and leapt across to the other car just as Hush's Colt roared. Touch the Sky's momentum threw him into the lead car hard. He recovered and instantly stooped behind the shelter of a seat back.

"Hush?"

"Yeah?"

"You get 'em?"

"I don't think so. I didn't really see him. I heard something."

"From which direction?"

"From every direction," the youth said miserably. "But he's here."

Touch the Sky felt the back of his neck tingling. His shaman sense verified Hush's words. Sis-ki-dee was there, all right, on that car, waiting to kill again.

"Sis-ki-dee!" Touch the Sky called out. "Tell me a thing! When you kill a sleeping child, do you boast and recite your coups? Do you dangle the scalp proudly?"

The faintest noise of mocking laughter answered Touch the Sky. The warrior poised himself like a listening bird, trying to use the sounds to locate his quarry. He signaled to Hush, telling him to stay back out of the way and watch the door nearest him.

"Tell me, Red Peril! Is it true what they say? Is it true that you are afraid of women and that your men take turns playing the squaw for you?"

Another sound came. Perhaps, Touch the Sky thought, it was a sharp intake of angry breath. Despite the fear steeling his muscles, the Cheyenne had to smile. Sis-ki-dee was indeed an insane killer. But like Wolf Who Hunts Smiling, he was easily goaded with certain topics.

The last noise had guided Touch the Sky farther forward. He saw young Spider Winslowe huddled with Mr. Wiggle-Wobble between the next pair of seats. Spotting the dummy made Touch the Sky recall Spider's remarkable talents.

Touch the Sky bent forward and whispered something in the boy's ear. Spider nodded. A moment later, an authoritative voice rang out from the spot where Touch the Sky guessed Sis-ki-dee was hiding, "The game's up. I see you!"

The startled Blackfoot leapt to the aisle and tore toward the door. Touch the Sky jumped at the same time that Hush stepped in front of him to shoot. Touch the Sky's feet tangled with the

Orphan Train

boy's, the pistol went off, and Sis-ki-dee rushed by even as Touch the Sky crashed to the floor. The Cheyenne managed one desperate swipe with his blade, raking it across the fleeing renegade's rib cage. His arms thus engaged in the attack, he smashed hard into the floor even as the bleeding Sis-ki-dee broke to safety.

Chapter Fourteen

"It is Sis-ki-dee!" Little Horse said in angry frustration, spotting the fleeing brave below. "But hold your fire, bucks. Already that fleet-footed sneak is out of range."

"What has he done now?" Two Twists said. "By now he must be trying to kill Touch the Sky. They have no more time for mere sport. Perhaps he just did."

"Someone got off a shot," Tangle Hair said. "But clearly Sis-ki-dee was not hit. I only hope it was not our comrade or one of those children."

"This situation cannot stand," Little Horse said. "I do not think we can stem one more charge if our enemy decides to mount one. I have only two shells left. Tangle Hair has nothing but a handful of arrows."

Orphan Train

"And down there," Two Twists said, "they are not eating. Do they have water? Brothers, do you remember when our tribe had the Mountain Fever? Remember how the children died first? My aunt told me that was because little ones need water more frequently than their elders. Even the healthy little ones need it. We know Touch the Sky can endure well without water. But what of those children?"

Clearly such talk deeply troubled Little Horse. The tough brave had few soft places in him, but one of them was children. "Those children must at least have some water. Tangle Hair, give me that bladder bag."

"Hold," Two Twists said. "Why do you rival Touch the Sky in hogging all the sport for yourself? You made the last ride. This trip is mine."

Little Horse mustered some of his usual bravado. "Why, listen to the dug sucker! Still dropping yellow pellets, and he wants to ride in Little Horse's stead! Will a pup stand in for a full-grown dog?"

"Pup!" Two Twists said. He was sensitive about being the youngest of them. "Who lifted his clout to torment the enemy when we fought Sis-ki-dee on Wendigo Mountain?"

"You did, buck. I was there and saw you. But see how it is? You too have had plenty of sport. Indeed, any brave who rides with Touch the Sky will seldom be without his battle kit. Now give over. This ride is mine."

Judd Cole

"Two Twists is right," Tangle Hair said. "Let one of us go. You have run the risk too many times. Never forget that the cup can go once too often to the well."

Little Horse laughed, reining his pony around for the charge and tying the bladder bag to his rope rigging.

"Risk? Brothers, risk is the ridge we live on! I have never hoped to die of old age in my tipi. If I do not ride back, I have only one request. When you place my things on my scaffold, place the Spanish dagger Touch the Sky gave me in my dead hand."

The stalwart brave slapped his piebald hard on the rump. Like an artillery round propelled from a rifled barrel, the Cheyenne pony hurtled once again down the steep slope.

"I'm awful damn sorry, Touch the Sky!" Hush said.

Touch the Sky's right cheek was already swelling from his hard collision with the floor. He pulled himself up and shook his head. "Wasn't your fault, Hush. We both got in each other's way at the wrong time. But I got a piece of him, at least, to remind him there's a price for dropping by without an invitation. More important, we scared him off the train."

"Think he'll be back?"

"Knowing him, I can only say I don't know. But my hunch is he won't. I don't know the schedule for this track. I know the railroad line to the south gets more traffic now. But there's got to be another train due through here. I don't think Siski-dee has enough time to play with us. If we—"

A fast, rolling beat of hooves sent both friends scrambling to the bullet-shattered windows.

"Aw, my God!" Hush shouted. "That crazy friend of yours is charging again!"

Down the slope Little Horse rushed, his braid streaming out behind him. The tough piebald leapt and turned, avoiding the deadly volley being raised by the renegades. Little Horse rose up for a moment, a half-full bladder bag dangling in his right hand. He whirled the bag around his head, flung it, and sent it thumping into the train coach.

The next moment, while a horrified Touch the Sky watched, Little Horse's pony took a hit to its right flank and buckled under the warrior. A moment later Little Horse was pinned down by withering fire. He huddled low behind his dead pony.

"He can't run to the train," Touch the Sky said. "It's too far across their best firing zone! He wouldn't get twenty feet."

Touch the Sky watched the plucky Little Horse snatch his shotgun from its boot and prepare to make his final stand. The cornered brave also had his bow to hand, though Touch the Sky could see he had few arrows.

"Courage, brother," Touch the Sky whispered,

reaching up to touch the grizzly claws dangling around his neck. But in fact Little Horse was in the same hurting place all of them were in—trapped like badgers in their holes, waiting only for the slaughter.

Little Horse was forced to flatten himself lower and lower as the enemy rounds searched him out. Over and over, his dead pony seemed to flinch as rounds pounded into her, giving her a jerky vitality. When a bullet creased his forehead, Little Horse felt warm blood trickling into his eyes.

With a great effort he was able to turn enough to glimpse the iron horse behind him. He'd be shot just trying to rise for the sprint.

There was nothing for it. He was caught between the sap and the bark. Any effort would only make him go farther to fare worse. Sometimes it was best to do nothing except patiently endure. Though secretly the tough-talking brave did fear death he would face it with a sneer of defiance on his lips even as the fatal blow fell. But that day was not a good day to die. It was a good day to fight well and save his brother and those children.

Another round whizzed by his head so close it sounded like a blow fly. Little Horse laid his weapons to hand and pressed himself even closer to his mother, the earth, raising a brief prayer to Maiyun, the Good Supernatural.

Orphan Train

* * *

"Brother," Tangle Hair said to Two Twists, "Little Horse is dead if we leave him there!"

The two braves were perched at the very edge of the ridge, ready to offer what fire they could if the renegades rushed Little Horse or the train. Surely, the charge must soon be coming.

Two Twists looked over his shoulder to the spot where their ponies were tethered behind them. His eye fell on the sabino pony Touch the Sky had given him—a light red with a white belly. The best pony in the entire Cheyenne common corral, as Two Twists himself had boasted.

"Yes," he said. "Little Horse may die. But not alone. Here, Tangle Hair. Take my rifle, and Maiyun guide your aim. I am riding down there to rescue Little Horse."

"Woman Face!" Wolf Who Hunts Smiling's voice said from the boulders behind the train. "Send those children out and you and your pathetic band may ride away from here!"

Those words immediately filled Touch the Sky with hope. He looked at Hush. "Perk up, fella. The stick might finally be floating our way."

"Whaddya mean? I couldn't figure out that damned caterwauling."

"That brave you just heard caterwauling in Cheyenne is not one to bargain. Yet he offered to bargain with me. I can trade my life for yours."

For a moment Hush narrowed his eyes suspiciously. "You gunna do it?"

Touch the Sky might have laughed had their situation not been so bleak. "I just might if you keep showing so little faith in your battle comrade."

"Sorry." Hush looked sheepish. "You've put your bacon in the fire for us already."

"For you, true enough. But also for my people. This crime is being pinned on my tribe, thanks to those red criminals out there right now. But if a hard, uncompromising man like Wolf Who Hunts Smiling is even pretending to offer a bargain, they must be running out of time. Somebody they won't be happy to see is coming."

"Woman Face! You will answer me or all face death!" Wolf Who Hunts Smiling said.

Touch the Sky again cast a worried glance toward Little Horse. Every so often, a renegade sent a bullet thwacking into the dead piebald. Little Horse could not even draw a deep breath for fear of exposing himself to fire. Clearly the renegades dearly hoped to ransom the children. That must be why, Touch the Sky thought, they were avoiding the rush. They knew an attack might kill too many children, and thus lower the overall profit.

"Is that you, Wolf Who Hunts Smiling?" Touch the Sky shouted back. "Pardon my delay in answering. I thought a horse whinneyed, but now I see it was nothing so important."

Then several children giggled until Touch the

Orphan Train

Sky said, "You kids quiet down."

"Okay," Hush said authoritatively. "Shut up. We got a war goin' on here!"

"Insults are nothing but words!" Wolf Who Hunts Smiling suddenly roared out in English. "And words are cheap, the coins spent freely by hoary-headed old women. Will you send out the children?"

"Yes," Touch the Sky said and Hush turned green until the warrior added, "when Pawnees are invited to dance with us!"

The exchange of insults was abruptly cut short when Two Twists, lashing his sabino pony with a light sisal whip, quartered along the face of the slope at a gallop, bearing for Little Horse's position. Touch the Sky knew the plan. Every man in his band had either been saved or saved another by the same method. The rider slid far forward, leaving room behind. Then he swung one hand down to the waiting man and pulled him up behind. Cheyennes practiced the movement, and indeed, in Touch the Sky's band the strategy was necessary often enough that practice was not needed.

The sabino performed marvelously, though it was not quite as adept at zigzagging as some ponies. Two Twists bore down, Little Horse leapt up, and their hands clasped. A shout of triumph went up from Touch the Sky and Hush.

A heartbeat later, a gout of blood erupted from Two Twists's left shoulder, and he flew hard from his pony leaving Little Horse clutching thin air.

Chapter Fifteen

"Sir, please send my unit up to Register Cliffs. Seth Carlson has had time to attack by now. But I had our telegrapher check with the Beardslee portable unit. No attack has commenced yet. Sir, I know you find it hard to believe, but I swear, on my honor as an officer and a gentleman, Seth Carlson is in cahoots with those criminal renegades!"

Tom Riley fell silent and stood by for the blast. But it never came. Col. Garret Peatross had finally shaken himself from his academic myopia long enough to notice a few things. Seth Carlson was a capable enough officer in terms of ability in the field. He had finished fifth in his class at West Point. A top shooter with the Spencer carbine, he was also an experienced tracker who often rode out without scouts. Yet lately, every time he was ordered to skirmish a few Indians, he found excuse after excuse for dawdling. That behavior seemed suspicious to Peatross. Maybe Carlson was in fact colluding with the enemy. More than one soldier had turned rotten chasing after money.

"He most definitely should have engaged the enemy by now," Peatross said. "If that ragtag militia band gets there first, they'll end up killing half the kids and making laughingstocks out of the army."

Riley leapt eagerly at the remark because Peatross had never before shown sympathy to his case. "Sir, my men are ready. I'm convinced the town of Bighorn Falls is secure. I've sent out three Gros Ventre scouts. Good trackers all, they've found no recent sign of any Indian activity."

Peatross frowned. The situation was a damned standoff. He trusted Riley to get the job done, all right. But what if that town was attacked again?

Reading concern in the Colonel's face, Riley said tactfully, "Sir? Just as a precaution, we could station a few squads of recruits in town for a show of force. Indians don't know trained soldiers from fresh fish. If they see enough bluecoats, they'll ride on."

Peatross seemed to take heart at the suggestion. He glanced down again at the *Register Gazette* that contained Nat Trilby's maudlin story. "Riley, you do have a level head in a scrape. This situation is an absolute priority. I take it you've heard about the telegram from G-3?"

Riley nodded solemnly, trying not to grin at Peatross's obvious worry. G-3 was the highest level of the War Department. And that terse telegram had not minced any words:

SAVE THOSE CHILDREN, AND QUICK!

"I suppose I could order Winslowe's dragoons into town," Peatross said.

"Fine idea, sir! They're good lads. And as soon as Winslowe relieves my platoon sergeant in town, we'd be free to ride north."

Peatross glanced at the newspaper once again, thought about that telegram, and debated no more. "Good luck, Riley. But for God's sake, man, hurry! Just make sure you do nothing to endanger those children further."

With the coming of darkness, Touch the Sky knew the final moments of the battle were at hand.

It had grown ominously quiet. Occasionally, rifles still cracked, pinning Little Horse and Two Twists behind the dead piebald. Other than that, and the occasional taunt from Wolf Who Hunts Smiling, Big Tree, or Sis-ki-dee, silence reigned.

The children had reached the ends of their tethers; several could do nothing but curl up and cry softly. Touch the Sky's heart broke to hear their sobbing. He felt a white-hot rage toward the monsters who could make little ones suffer so.

Touch the Sky moved as close as he dared to a window and called out softly, taking advantage of the quiet, "Little Horse?"

"I have ears, buck."

"And a stout heart, also. How fares it, Cheyenne? Can you hear me, also, Two Twists?"

"Why would I not?" Two Twists said. "Was I not born with ears?"

Touch the Sky grinned. If any band every showed more spirit in the teeth of disaster, he had never crossed their trail. Yet he could not help feeling a sharp lance point of worry. Young Two Twists had put up a good show, but his voice had sounded weak and dangerously close to unconsciousness.

"Brother, our double-braided young bull has seriously damaged a horn," Little Horse said. "I have tied off his wound, but he is pouring blood. We have no time to discuss the causes of the wind."

Touch the Sky felt his heart sink. Little Horse would not say so openly, but he was hinting to Touch the Sky that Two Twists would soon die unless some reckless plan were put in motion.

Two Twists was not so far gone that he was fooled. "No hurry, bucks. I have a soft place under me here and the makings for a white man's cigarette. I would like to enjoy a smoke before you force me to action again."

Then a child's pitiful cry rose for a moment,

Judd Cole

sad, plaintive notes, pushing Touch the Sky to come up with a plan to save his band and the innocent children.

"Have ears," Big Tree said. He looked at Sis-ki-dee and Wolf Who Hunts Smiling crouched on either side of him in their emergency council. "Night has fallen. This is our last chance. Carlson must rescue the children in the morning if we cannot spirit them away sooner. We may not even have that much time if the foolish hair-face militia blunders onto us sooner."

"My people will not move tonight," Wolf Who Hunts Smiling said. "They will not go out from camp after dark."

"You dog-eating Cheyennes have many womanly customs," Big Tree said with contempt. "But I have no desire to remain here any longer. Sis-ki-dee has had his chance to sneak aboard and kill the Bear Caller. He failed. But we Comanches invented the art of stealth. Once before I sneaked up on this White Man Runs Him. I skewered him with a special Long Arrow tipped in white man's sheet iron."

"So you did," Wolf Who Hunts Smiling said. "But did it kill him?"

"Your words fly straight. It did not. That is why I want this chance now. Give it to me. If I fail as did Sis-ki-dee, never mind charging the iron horse. We will follow Wolf Who Hunts Smiling's plan and use the thunder pack to kill all of them.

Orphan Train

Even if the shaman again miraculously survives, the deaths of so many paleface whelps, pinned to his tipi entrance, will ensure his banishment from both the white and red nations."

Wolf Who Hunts Smiling considered this, then nodded. Sis-ki-dee followed suit.

"But if you fail," Wolf Who Hunts Smiling said, again hoisting the canvas-covered nitro pack tied to his pony, "we wait no longer."

"They'll make their move tonight," Touch the Sky said. "They have to. Time is working against them."

"But what move?" Hush said. "How come they don't just rush the train?"

"They might do that. Or they might try to kill me. But don't forget they know damn well some of them are going to die before they get past Little Horse and Two Twists, even if Two Twists is wounded. Whatever they do, it'll come with darkness."

From their cramped positions in the aisle, the two friends craned their necks to gauge the depth of the night. Again a full moon shone from a starshot sky, providing plenty of light. Touch the Sky wasn't sure whether that light would work for them or against them.

"Woman Face! If you love your loyal followers so much, why not break from cover to save them? Do you know, shaman, I think that bullet I put in Two Twists has killed him by now. But surely he died singing the praises of the tall one who not only got him killed, but left him to die!"

"Do not build my scaffold yet, wily wolf!" Two Twists said from out of the night. "I do not plan on crossing over until I have spit in your dead face!"

"Bear Caller!" Sis-ki-dee roared out. "That child whose throat I cut thanks you, too, for saving him!"

"Damn them!" Hush said.

"They're just goading me. That's what bothers me." Touch the Sky glanced nervously around. "I've got a hunch they're distracting me."

"From what?"

"I hope I'm wrong," Touch the Sky muttered in English to Hush before calling out to the renegades: "I have heard my close friends Wolf Who Hunts Smiling and Sis-ki-dee. But why have I not heard from the Comanche terror, Big Tree? Speak to me, Quohada! Tell me again how you topped my woman and made her scream like a banshee!"

Dead silence greeted his taunt. Then, faintly, a muffled thump came from the top of the coach.

"You want to hear from me?" Big Tree said from very close by. "Then hear this, White Man Runs Him. The unborn child we just ripped from your squaw's womb was a son!"

Touch the Sky's blood stopped and seemed to flow backward in his veins. For a long moment, a dizzying rush of spinning blackness surrounded him; within him there surged a welling of fear mingled with unbelievable rage. But how could they know about his child?

It couldn't be true, he tried to convince himself. But if it were? If they had done this heinous thing? Oh, if they had—

Abruptly, Touch the Sky's pulse quit throbbing in his palms and his breathing calmed. He shook Hush by the shoulder, pointed overhead, then put his fingers to his lips.

Touch the Sky let himself silently out onto the platform. He could see Little Horse and Two Twists in the moonlight, still hunkered behind the dead piebald. Little Horse held his shotgun, ready to die fighting.

Touch the Sky gripped the metal rungs of the ladder and climbed up until he could peer over the top of the car. The moment he did, he saw Big Tree crouched at the opposite end, preparing to lower himself onto the front platform!

Moving with incredible speed, Touch the Sky slid his knife from his sash and whipped it hard in a fast overhand throw. He had the satisfaction of seeing it embed itself in the meaty portion of Big Tree's right shoulder. But the huge Quohada Comanche barely flinched as he dropped out of sight down the ladder.

Then Touch the Sky made a crucial mistake. Realizing he was caught, Big Tree had decided to simply take his chances on foot outside the train, racing back toward his position in the rocks. After all, the two stranded Cheyennes were in front of him and off to the left and would not notice him. Hoping that Little Horse could stop Big Tree with a shot, Touch the Sky cried out, "Little Horse! Eyes right and behind!"

Little Horse glanced back as told, spotted their enemy, and swung the muzzle of his shotgun around. But he was not within effective range. His spray of buckshot did manage to pepper Big Tree's face with tiny wounds, but did not stop him.

Then Touch the Sky's stomach dropped when Big Tree, enraged by the two wounds, avoided Little Horse's next shot by diving onto the coach with the children!

Screams came from below, followed by a curse from Hush and the roar of his Colt Navy pistol. Moments later, a cry of pain rose from Hush and the children screamed more.

Staving off panic, Touch the Sky scrambled down the ladder, flung open the back door, and leapt into the coach just in time to see Big Tree hurtling down the aisle toward him, a long Mexican bayonet aimed at his vitals.

Wolf Who Hunts Smiling and Sis-ki-dee heard the racket all around them as they worked quickly in the darkness. With Big Tree distracting Woman Face, it had been a simple matter to sneak up to the coach from the opposite side.

"What is happening?" Sis-ki-dee whispered

after the gunshot and the screams.

"It matters not," Wolf Who Hunts Smiling said. "If Big Tree emerges alive, those children are ours. If not, they will soon belong to their white God!"

Wolf Who Hunts Smiling finished placing the nitro pack against a wheel of the coach, positioning it so that one shot would send everyone in that coach, including Woman Face, across the Great Divide.

Chapter Sixteen

Big Tree was without doubt one of the most formidable warriors of the entire red nation. A giant among Indians, he had defeated even the legendary Apache, Stone Mountain, in wrestling. The sight of that blood-crazed killing machine with Touch the Sky's knife still protruding from his shoulder and face spotted with blood could strike fear into a grizzly.

But Big Tree, too, had made a serious mistake. He could not resist goading Touch the Sky about the one thing that was sure to cut him hard: Honey Eater and her no-longer-secret child. And that remark had finally struck all fear from Touch the Sky. In its place was a white-hot need to kill his enemies.

In the moments before Big Tree reached him,

Orphan Train

Touch the Sky saw Hush lying in the aisle, blood pouring from a deep gash to his temple. Hush's shot had missed once again, but far more experienced men had failed to kill this Comanche devil.

Then his hurtling enemy was atop him, and Touch the Sky gave over from thinking to pure action. He fell backward, in the direction of Big Tree's attack, using his enemy's momentum against him. Touch the Sky stuck both feet up at an angle, caught Big Tree in the chest, and with a powerful tensing of his thighs, lifted his enemy off the floor and up over him.

Big Tree went airborne for perhaps ten feet, crashing hard into the rear door of the coach. But Touch the Sky was on his back, and he lost valuable time scrambling around to his feet. He had not quite fought his way up when the huge renegade crashed down onto him, snarling like an enraged wolverine.

The sheer weight alone thumped all the air from his lungs. But Touch the Sky, like any experienced fighter, knew that most fights eventually end up on the ground; thus, he had practiced ground-fighting techniques. So rather than fight for air, he let his chest flatten completely under the huge weight. That move brought him face-to-face with one of his most hated enemies in the world.

The sudden flip had surprised Big Tree. His eyes, two dead chips of flint, looked at the Cheyenne with the cunning hatred of a snake. But before Big Tree could move, Touch the Sky brought one arm behind his neck and one knee in front of it. Suddenly flexing forward with his arm, outward with his knee, Touch the Sky applied an excruciating choke hold to the Comanche. The massive and instant pressure cut off both air and blood. Within just moments, Big Tree's weight began to slacken.

Touch the Sky lost control of the hold when the big man fell to one side of him. The Cheyenne instantly gripped his knife for the death plunge, but that delay was all Big Tree needed to thrust his bayonet at Touch the Sky's stomach.

The Cheyenne slammed down with his left arm, blocking and thrusting in one movement. For a moment, he drove the bigger man's arm off target. But a heartbeat later, Big Tree and Touch the Sky were locked in a deadly standoff. Big Tree could not get the blade into him, and Touch the Sky could not drive his knife without losing control of Big Tree's blade hand. Big Tree's jaw muscles, only a gnat's width from Touch the Sky's face, bunched tight as he strained to drive steel.

"I bulled her before I cut your whelp from her!" Big Tree said in a strained whisper, and those words cost him the fight.

Strength that was physical, shamanic, and pure anger-driven surged into Touch the Sky as if lightning had struck him. He roared deep in his chest; the very sound hurt Big Tree. Then the big Comanche was thrown off so mightily that he shattered two of the seats behind him when he landed.

Hush saw Big Tree slam into the seats. Hoping to finish off the job, Hush cocked back his right hand and flung the Colt Navy revolver at the savage intruder. Unfortunately, he let if fly precisely as the bellowing Touch the Sky leapt up to finish his enemy.

The heavy six-shooter thunked hard into Touch the Sky's skull, just above his left ear, and Touch the Sky staggered. He fought to finish his charge, but the blow stunned his nervous system. Hush groaned with fearful misery when the Cheyenne slumped to his knees, struggling to remain conscious.

Big Tree, shaking his head like a confused bull, regained sense enough to grin at his good fortune. He picked up his bayonet and struggled to his feet.

"Kids!" Mr. Wiggle-Wobble screamed. "He's gonna kill Touch the Sky! Charge!"

Enough butterflies, according to one Indian proverb, could kill a man. Big Tree almost discovered the certain truth of that wisdom when the frightened but determined group of children slammed into him.

Hush lowered his head like a bull and slammed it into Big Tree's midsection. As Big Tree sucked in hard and bent forward, Tommy

Judd Cole

Truesdale kicked upward with all his might, driving the toes of his boots into Big Tree's nose. Before the renegade could recover, Sarah Pettigrew managed to scratch one of his eyeballs deep with little but deadly fingers.

Big Tree's roar of pain jogged Touch the Sky back to partial awareness. Though he could not recover in time to sink his blade into the fleeing Comanche, he had the satisfaction of seeing those supposed helpless white children send perhaps the meanest renegade on the Plains fleeing into the night.

"Chase him!" Hush screamed. "No!" Touch the Sky said. "Hush, you damned fool! You kids did good. But don't get victory fever and make stupid mistakes. They'll cut you down quick if you show yourself out there in that moonlight. Just be glad that red devil is gone."

Just then Little Horse cried out from his exposed position, "Brother! Trouble plenty besides what just ran off that train! I see, under the wheeled lodge, Wolf Who Hunts Smiling and Siski-dee placing something. You know full well they are not digging a fire pit! Brother, you and those children must get off that train! Now!"

"Eat more strong mushrooms, stout warrior, before you give me more such good advice! Shall I paint spots on them for targets, too, so the renegades will have sport when they shoot them?"

The horrible dilemma was clear to all in Touch the Sky's band. Touch the Sky and the orphans could stay on that train and risk death at any moment by explosion, or they could flee and risk being cut down by bullets.

But there was no choice, and Touch the Sky knew it. He would be killed, of course, if they detrained. But the children might live. Otherwise, Wolf Who Hunts Smiling meant to take an ugly revenge.

"All right, kids!" Touch the Sky said. "Never mind your stuff. Just follow me!"

He switched to Cheyenne. "Wolf Who Hunts Smiling!"

"You know my name. Say what you will."

"I am bringing the children. Hold your fire."

After a long pause, Touch the Sky heard his enemy's barely restrained mirth as he said, "Come out then. No one will hurt you."

Tom Riley and his platoon had surprised Seth Carlson and his men in a holding camp about a mile back from the Kansas-Pacific tracks. Leaving a guard to make sure there were witnesses to any further treason, they raced on toward the besieged children. They were still at least a quarter mile from the site of the train derailment when the single shot rang out.

Riley cursed. His men were formed in sets of four, butts of their Spencer carbines resting on their thighs or their saddle trees.

"Cunningham! Majors! Boone! Maddox! Front and center!"

Riley had a fast sorrel, as did all of those men, the fastest riders in his unit. Ordering the men to ride with him and the rest to follow as quickly as possible, Riley gave hard spur to his mount and led his men toward the moonwashed headland.

"Focus down to nothing but your target!" Riley said. "Stay frosty and shoot plumb on my command. Make every shot for score!"

Riley led them over the last ridge and saw in the ample moonlight the disabled train, Touch the Sky and the orphans filing out of the coach, two more Indians huddled behind a dead pony, another watching from the ridge, rifle at the ready—and all those braves massed a bit farther back, evidently about to open fire on Touch the Sky and the children. Riley was also quick to spot Wolf Who Hunts Smiling and Sis-ki-dee, enemies well known to him, huddled at the opposite side of the train, aiming rifles at it.

Riley couldn't know yet exactly what the two renegades were aiming at. But instinct made him squeeze off his first rounds in that direction instead of toward the larger group of braves. Only later would he learn that his timely decision had saved not only his friend, but all of the kids, who were still far too close to the tracks to miss the brunt of any nitro explosion.

When one of the soldier's shots ripped a hole through the buckskin sheath of Sis-ki-dee's North & Savage .44, Sis-ki-dee and Wolf Who

Orphan Train

Hunts Smiling made their break for it. Riley's sharpshooters, meantime, opened fire on the mass of the renegades. The arrival of honest bluecoats was the final straw. An ear-to-ear grin split Riley's face as the denizens of the Renegade Nation scattered in confused disarray.

"Brothers," Touch the Sky said, "I have learned to fear the blue blouses as much as any Cheyenne must. Yet I confess no sight was more welcome, as I climbed off that train, than Tom Riley and his troopers opening fire on the renegades."

Several sleeps had passed since the incident near Register Cliffs. Touch the Sky, Honey Eater, and Touch the Sky's loyal band sat around the fire pit in his tipi—though the fire was kept low, and blankets sewn to the tipi cover were intended to minimize shadow targets.

"Sioux scouts brought in a copy of the white man's newspaper," Touch the Sky said. "Hush Cochran was injured, but he will recover. He is being treated as a hero for protecting the littler ones. This white scrivener, Nat Trilby, did much to help us. Thanks to him, those children on the train not only received a military escort for the rest of their journey; they have become famous in the eyes of the hair faces. The best families in the West are fighting to raise them."

"Good. And all is well here." Little Horse's eyes cut briefly toward Honey Eater. But then the stout warrior frowned. "That is, as well as things can be in a camp divided against itself."

Touch the Sky nodded, taking his full meaning. Little Horse was right. Touch the Sky had indeed taken time out to thank Maiyun when he had found Honey Eater unharmed. But somehow, their enemies knew about the child growing inside of her, and they feared that child as much as they feared Touch the Sky himself.

Two Twists moved somewhat stiffly when Tangle Hair passed him the pipe. His arm was still tied in soft doeskin dressings. "I have not forgotten your vision, brother, which showed blood on our sacred arrows. We beat these renegades again. But each fight gets harder as they get stronger."

No one said anything. Indeed, what was there to say? His words were true, and they were strong enough to accept the truth.

Touch the Sky looked at his beautiful woman in the soft light, and his heart swelled with love for her and the life growing in her. He vowed again that nothing or no one would hurt them. And he reminded himself of the hardest truth an Indian must learn: Life meant being a warrior, and the end of one battle only marked the beginning of the next.